DEDICATION

To my sister, Yi-Hwa

PENELOPE SWAN

Darcy Revealed

A Pride and Prejudice Variation

PENELOPE SWAN

OTHER BOOKS BY PENELOPE SWAN:

The Dark Darcy series:

- The Netherfield Affair (Book 1)
- Intrigue at the Ball (Book 2)
- The Poisoned Proposal (Book 3)
- Secrets at Pemberley (Book 4)

CONTENTS

CHAPTER ONE 1
CHAPTER TWO 11
CHAPTER THREE 21
CHAPTER FOUR 29
CHAPTER FIVE 36
CHAPTER SIX 45
CHAPTER SEVEN 55
CHAPTER EIGHT 63
CHAPTER NINE...73
CHAPTER TEN 81
CHAPTER ELEVEN 88
CHAPTER TWELVE 98
CHAPTER THIRTEEN 109
CHAPTER FOURTEEN......................................116
CHAPTER FIFTEEN 125
CHAPTER SIXTEEN 133
CHAPTER SEVENTEEN 142
CHAPTER EIGHTEEN.......................................152
CHAPTER NINETEEN 161
CHAPTER TWENTY 168
CHAPTER TWENTY-ONE 179
CHAPTER TWENTY-TWO..................................187
CHAPTER TWENTY-THREE..............................196
OTHER BOOKS BY THIS AUTHOR: 204
ABOUT THE AUTHOR 213
ACKNOWLEDGEMENTS....................................214

PENELOPE SWAN

CHAPTER ONE

"If we do not leave soon, we shall be late."

Elizabeth Bennett glanced at her Aunt Gardiner who was looking worriedly at the clock on the wall. They had been in the boutique far longer than they had anticipated. There had been so many beautiful items—from cashmere shawls and ivory fans to silk gowns and fine wool pelisses—that they had quite forgotten the time as they admired the things put on display in front of them.

Elizabeth's home town of Meryton in the Hertfordshire countryside had only a small milliner's and fabric shop, which hardly gave a glimpse into the latest fashions. So it had been a rare treat to explore the range of shopping that London had to offer. And Madame Lemaine's was reputed to be the best.

The best and the most expensive too, Elizabeth thought wryly. Indeed, she and her sister, Jane had only a meagre allowance of £50 a year, which could barely stretch to a few of the luxurious items in this shop. But it was still lovely to admire and dream. As it was, they had already made a number of small purchases—having been tempted far beyond their budget—and were even now awaiting the final alterations to an elegant cornflower-blue gown that was meant for Jane.

"I am very sorry, Aunt, that we should be late on my account," said Jane, her face contrite.

"Oh, my dear, I should not worry if it were simply for ourselves. It is only because I have promised Mrs Needham that we would be at the Clarendon Hotel at four o'clock for Afternoon Tea and I should hate to break my word."

"It should not be much longer," said Elizabeth hopefully, watching the seamstress's needle flash across the fabric. She turned to glance idly at the table next to them, where several other dresses were awaiting alterations, and noticed a gown of the most beautiful shell-pink, trimmed with delicate white lace and tiny seed pearls that shimmered on the bodice. "Oh, look, Jane—is that not the handsomest gown you have ever seen?"

"Indeed," Jane agreed, reaching out to caress the fabric reverently. Her fingers came across a tag between the soft folds and she read the inscription. "Oh, it is addressed to Georgiana Darcy, Lizzy... Do you think that could be Mr Darcy's sister?"

Mrs Gardiner nodded. "It is possible that there is another lady who bears the same name, but I think it highly unlikely. Madame Lemaine's shop is patronised by the wealthiest and most influential in society—and I imagine that the Darcys are her regular customers. That gown is certainly one of the most luxurious I have ever seen."

"Mr Darcy must dote on his sister, to purchase such a gown for her," said Jane with a smile.

Elizabeth did not say anything. She could never think of Darcy without a prickle of irritation. She recalled their last meeting at the Netherfield ball. Why had he asked her to dance, only to remain stiff and silent throughout most of it? And when she had challenged him about his behaviour towards poor Mr Wickham, he had responded with haughty indifference. Oh, just thinking of it made her temper rise! She had never met another man who vexed her so.

To be sure, Mr Darcy was extremely attractive and Elizabeth had to grudgingly admit that she had not met a man his equal in physical perfection. There were none as tall and handsome, with such a fine figure and such a commanding presence. Something about him had drawn her to him—as it had drawn the gaze of every other woman in the room—when she first met him.

Elizabeth sighed inwardly. If she was honest with herself, she had to admit that part of the reason for her hostility was because she had been slighted by Mr Darcy when they first met. Her pride had been wounded. She still bristled when she recalled his dismissive comment:

"She is tolerable but not handsome enough to tempt me."

The arrogance of such a comment had immediately set her feelings against him. However, she had been surprised to find on subsequent meetings that he seemed to pay her particular attention—that often she would glance up to find Darcy's eyes upon her. She had been puzzled by his behaviour. She knew he did not admire her so why did he look at her? *No doubt he watches me only to find more flaws in me to criticise*, Elizabeth thought, her mouth tightening with annoyance.

She was brought out of her thoughts by the proprietor of the store, Madame Lemaine, coming across to speak to them. The elegant French woman was obviously wearing one of her own creations and Elizabeth eyed her silk crepe gown with admiration.

"*Excusez-moi*, madame," she addressed Mrs Gardiner. "I could not help overhearing your conversation just now. If you and the mademoiselles need to leave first, that is no problem. I can arrange for my delivery boy to conduct the parcels to your residence later this afternoon when they are ready."

"Really?" said Mrs Gardiner in delight. "That is extremely kind of you, Madame Lemaine!"

"Think nothing of it," said Madame Lemaine. "It is a service I frequently provide for my customers. As you can imagine, many of them come to London on shopping excursions and are keen to spend their time more wisely than waiting in a store. This way, they are free to go on and visit other shops, whilst my seamstresses finish the necessary work."

Mrs Gardiner inclined her head. "It is a most ideal solution. We shall take you up on your kind offer, Madame. Come, Jane and Lizzy—if we leave now, we should still be able to arrive punctually."

They hurried from the shop and found a hackney cab to take them to the Clarendon Hotel. Elizabeth looked around with interest as they entered the elegant institution. Clarendon's was well known for its French chef, who was a former servant of King Louis

XVIII—indeed, it was often said that the Clarendon's was the only place where a genuine French meal could be had.

They found Mrs Needham waiting for them in the beautiful little tea room off the main lobby and sat down together with her. A tea service in fine bone china was served, together with dainty little cakes, thin bread and butter, hot buttered scones and crumpets, cucumber sandwiches, French biscuits, and a bowl of ripe, red strawberries accompanied by a jug of rich cream. Elizabeth had to agree, after sampling the delicious treats, that the hotel's culinary reputation was well deserved.

"And have you heard the news?" Mrs Needham asked them excitedly. "Mary King's grandfather has passed away and left her a fortune of ten thousand pounds. She is a veritable heiress now!"

"Indeed?" said Mrs Gardiner. "How fortunate for her. I do not know the girl well, but Jane, you and Lizzy must have made her acquaintance, for her uncle lives not far from Meryton."

"Yes, we have met Miss King a few times, though we do not know her very well yet," said Jane. "I believe that she only entered society recently, for she is still just sixteen and, until now, has been living very quietly under her uncle's guardianship."

"Well, now that she is an heiress, life certainly will not be quiet anymore," said Elizabeth with a chuckle. "Perhaps her uncle might even allow her to come to London and make her debut."

Finally, the enjoyable tête-à-tête came to an end and they returned to the Gardiners' modest residence in Gracechurch Street. Elizabeth was delighted to see, upon their return, that the packages from the shop had already been delivered. Together with Jane, she collected all the parcels and bore them to the bedroom they shared.

"You must try on your new gown this instant, Jane," she said enthusiastically, taking hold of the largest parcel which was addressed to her sister. "I should like to see how it looks on you, now that the alterations have been made. I believe it will be the most elegant gown you have ever owned."

Jane came and stood by her, watching eagerly as Elizabeth ripped open the packet. However, as she pulled back the brown paper, Elizabeth paused in confusion. The folds of cloth revealed were not a soft cornflower-blue but a pale shell-pink.

"Oh—that is not my gown!" cried Jane.

"Indeed, it is not," Elizabeth agreed. "This looks like the gown for Georgiana Darcy. Do you think there has been a mistake?" She turned the parcel over to look at the outside again. Clearly written in bold, black writing was Jane's name and their aunt's address. Elizabeth frowned. "It is definitely addressed to you."

She turned the packet over again and carefully lifted out the soft bundle. Her eyes caught the sight of a piece of paper tucked amongst the folds. She extracted this slowly. It was a copy of the receipt and as she unfolded it and saw Darcy's sister's name, her suspicions were confirmed.

"I imagine that in the rush to get things packed and delivered, there must have been a mistake and the contents of the parcels were swapped. I wonder if Miss Darcy has received your gown?"

"Oh dear," said Jane. "What a muddle. What are we to do?"

"I suppose we shall have to inform Madame Lemaine about the mix-up and ask her to return this gown to its rightful owner," Elizabeth said. "Otherwise, we shall have to inform the Darcys ourselves. I imagine that they are at staying at their townhouse. I do not know if we could write to Miss Darcy directly as we have not been introduced; perhaps it would require our uncle to write to Mr Darcy." Elizabeth made a face. "I should dislike having to contact that gentleman."

Jane looked at her in mild surprise. "Lizzy, why do you dislike Mr Darcy so? I own, he can be a bit taciturn at times, but I imagine that it is simply his manner and no indication of his character."

"You are too good, Jane," said Elizabeth, shaking her head. "But I have long decided that Mr Darcy is the most disagreeable man I have ever had the misfortune to meet and I should be very glad to have nothing else to do with him. In any case, even if we were to contact him, I doubt he would lower himself to any connections with people on this side of town." She gave a mocking smile. "I would imagine that Mr Darcy has instructed his butler to refuse all correspondence from Cheapside and would disapprove of his footmen sullying their feet by coming here to retrieve the parcel."

Jane shook her head. "I think you are being unjust to Mr Darcy, Lizzy. But very well— perhaps the best course of action would be to contact Madame Lemaine and ask her to organise an exchange." Jane sighed. "Oh dear... It will mean asking our aunt and uncle to send one of their servants back to Madame Lemaine's shop with a message about the mix-up and I should not like to trouble them. They have been excessively kind already to provide so much transport and chaperonage for us while we are in town."

"I agree," said Elizabeth. "But it cannot be helped. We shall have to trespass on their kindness a little further. Perhaps we could broach the topic at the dinner table tonight."

CHAPTER TWO

In actual fact, Elizabeth was wrong about Darcy's reaction. Indeed, he was surprised by his own reaction when he learned from his sister that the package delivered to her had contained the wrong gown. When she told him it had come with another parcel, which was addressed to Miss Elizabeth Bennet, he had been uncomfortably aware of how his pulse had jumped at the sound of that name.

Darcy had been attempting unsuccessfully to put the beautiful, spirited Elizabeth from his mind ever since leaving Hertfordshire. After all, there was no question of him offering for her. The difference in their backgrounds and family positions should have precluded the possibility entirely, not to mention the complete want of propriety in so many members of her family.

Still... Darcy had been unable to put Elizabeth completely from his mind. Thoughts of her had persisted in tormenting him: fragments of conversations they had had at the Netherfield ball... the feel of her hand in his as they danced... the sparkle of laughter in those fine eyes when she had found something amusing... Somehow, no other woman had captivated him like this before.

He glanced down at the package that his sister had placed in front of him. And now here was an opportunity for him to see her again.

"Fancy Madame Lemaine making a mistake like that!" said Georgiana as she stood next to him. "What shall we do, Fitzwilliam? Should we return to Madame's shop with the wrong packages and ask her to deliver them to these young ladies? And I wonder if they might have my gown? Oh, I did so want to wear it for the soirée!"

Darcy knew what they should do, but suddenly it was as if his body had been separated from his mind, and his heart was directing his actions. He opened his mouth and was surprised at the words which came out:

"I am acquainted with these young ladies—I met them during my stay with Bingley in Hertfordshire. I believe this is the address for their uncle's residence in Cheapside; they must be in town and staying with their relatives in

Gracechurch Street." He nodded at Georgiana. "You may leave it with me. I shall send a servant there now with a note enquiring about the packages—and also your gown."

Georgiana gave him a puzzled look and Darcy thought she would ask him why he did not simply send the servant with the packages themselves. But luckily she did not voice the question. Though Georgiana had a lively disposition and could even be slightly defiant at times, she was also more than ten years his junior and well used to obeying him.

Indeed, most women of his acquaintance hardly ever questioned him—they simpered and fawned over him and could not please him enough. It was not until he met Elizabeth that Darcy realised how much he detested all that submissive adulation. Elizabeth was the first woman to challenge him and she had bewitched him with her playful impertinence and fiery intelligence. He glanced down at the package again and smiled to himself. Suddenly, he could not wait to see her again.

When Jane and Elizabeth sat down to dinner that evening with their aunt and uncle, Mrs Gardiner asked her husband if he would be making his customary trip to his warehouses the next morning.

"No, my dear, for I shall have a visitor tomorrow morning. Mr Darcy means to call upon us."

"Mr Darcy!" said Elizabeth in surprise, clattering her fork against her dish. "Coming here?"

Her uncle glanced at her. "Yes. I believe that he is in possession of some packages which should have been delivered to you and Jane. His note asks if he might call and bring the packages, and in the process, retrieve the one that was meant for his sister."

"But why should Mr Darcy come and do that himself?" wondered Elizabeth. "Surely he could simply send a servant?"

Mr Gardiner shrugged. "One does not wonder at the whims of great men. Perhaps he is bored and fancies a trip to Cheapside," he said with a humorous look.

Elizabeth shook her head. "It does not make sense..."

Mrs Gardiner looked speculatively at her nieces. It certainly did not make sense for Mr Darcy to come on the errand himself—unless he was keen to have the opportunity of meeting one of her nieces. She had not missed the fact that though Elizabeth often spoke of him in dismissive terms, her niece became very animated whenever she did speak of that gentleman. There seemed to be a great strength of feeling there, although whether that feeling was all animosity as Elizabeth claimed, it was hard to tell. In any case, Mrs Gardner decided that it would not hurt for the ladies to remain home the next morning and take the opportunity of meeting the visitor.

Accordingly, the next morning, the ladies sat in the pretty parlour overlooking the street. Jane was working on a piece of embroidery and Mrs Gardner was writing a letter, whilst Elizabeth was attempting to read a novel. However, she was vexed to find that her mind kept straying from the page. Indeed, it strayed in the most unusual direction—towards a tall, arrogant gentleman with piercing dark eyes and haughty manners. She found that she was listening constantly for the sound of a carriage drawing up outside the house and berated herself for her preoccupation. Surely she was not anticipating the arrival of Mr Darcy?

At last, the sound that Elizabeth had been listening for came from outside. Mrs Gardiner got up and walked over to look out the windows, whilst Elizabeth forced herself not to follow her aunt's example.

"Ah... it is Mr Darcy," said Mrs Gardiner. She turned and made swiftly for the hallway. "I shall go and ask if he would like to come and take tea with us in the parlour instead of seeing your uncle in his study. After all, it is only polite to offer him refreshment after the trouble he has taken to come here."

Elizabeth looked at her aunt in surprise, but before she had time to reflect further, Mr Darcy was at the parlour door. Elizabeth rose hurriedly and curtsied as the tall gentleman was escorted into the room by her aunt and uncle.

"Miss Bennet. Miss Elizabeth Bennett." Darcy swept them an elegant bow, then seated himself on one of the settees.

"Mr Darcy, we are honoured to welcome you to our humble abode," said Mrs Gardiner.

"The honour is mine," said Darcy quickly. "I apologise for the intrusion, but I felt that it was imperative to deliver these parcels as quickly as possible. My sister impressed upon me the urgency with which young ladies need to receive their latest purchases," he said with a slight smile as he indicated the two brown parcels he had brought with him.

Elizabeth stared at him in astonishment. She had never heard him speak with such civility nor conduct himself in such an unassuming manner.

Jane reached out to take the packages from Mr Darcy and pulled back the brown paper to check the contents. "Oh, yes... it is my gown... and this is the shawl that you purchased, Lizzy." She turned and picked up another parcel on the side table, passing it over to Mr Darcy. "And I believe this is your sister's gown, Mr Darcy."

Darcy gave the contents of the package a cursory glance. "Yes, I believe it is so. Georgiana will be pleased to have it ready for the soirée we are hosting tomorrow night at Darcy House."

"I am sure she will look delightful in it," said Jane with a smile.

Elizabeth was aware of Darcy's eyes upon her and given that she was the only person who had not yet spoken, she felt obliged to make a comment. "Is Miss Darcy enjoying her stay in London?" she asked.

"Yes, though I believe she found it a trifle lonely at first. She was used to her circle of friends back at my estate in Derbyshire. But luckily our neighbour, Mrs St John, has had a young relative come to stay with her from the countryside and, in the past few weeks, my sister and Miss St John have become firm friends. Miss St John is a few years older than Georgiana, but they are very alike in temperament. They have been delightful companions for each other and it has helped to make Georgiana's time in town far more enjoyable."

"That is good to hear," said Elizabeth. "And it is certainly true that having a good friend can make a trying experience far easier to endure—as I am sure you'll agree, Mr Darcy, given your recent stay in the countryside," she added with a teasing smile.

Darcy looked amused. "I assure you, Miss Bennet, I did not find my stay in Hertfordshire as unpleasant as you seem to imply. However, I fully admit that it was greatly enhanced by the pleasure of Bingley's company."

As he mentioned his friend, Darcy glanced at Jane, and Elizabeth wondered if he realised how disappointed her sister had been when they learned that Bingley had quit Netherfield so suddenly after the ball. Instead of the marriage proposal that everyone had been expecting, Jane had been left feeling abandoned, bewildered, and unsure of Bingley's intentions.

Jane coloured uncomfortably and looked away, as if aware of their thoughts. Elizabeth wondered if Bingley realised they were in town. She knew that Jane had written to Caroline Bingley, but had not had a reply from the lady as yet. She longed to ask Darcy about his friend, but she did not want to upset Jane. Instead, she let the subject drop and sat back as her uncle engaged Darcy in conversation.

Elizabeth was surprised again to observe Darcy responding in kind and completely without hauteur or disdain. He chatted amicably with her uncle, talking of fishing, hunting, and travel—in which they shared a mutual interest and enjoyment. She was pleased to note that with every expression and every sentence he uttered, her uncle showed his intelligence, his taste, and his good manners. It was immensely gratifying to know that Darcy would at last see she had some relations for whom there was no need to blush.

At length, Darcy stood up to take his leave. As he was bending over her hand, he looked into her eyes and said, "It has been a pleasure to meet you again, Miss Bennet."

Elizabeth knew not how to answer this. She did not feel that she could reply in kind—and yet she was surprised to discover that she had enjoyed his visit far more than she had expected.

Darcy smiled slightly. "Will you allow me, or do I ask too much, to introduce my sister to your acquaintance during your stay in London?"

Elizabeth stared at him in astonishment. His wish of introducing his sister to her was a compliment of the highest kind. In spite of her professed antagonism towards him, she was pleased and flattered. "Thank you, I should like that very much," she said.

Darcy's smile deepened and she felt her heart give a little jolt as she saw the warmth in his eyes. He turned towards her aunt and uncle. "Perhaps I might take this opportunity to invite you all to the soirée at Darcy House tomorrow night? It is merely a small affair with a few close friends—amongst them, some who claim an acquaintance with you: Mr Bingley and his sisters—but it should be an entertaining evening."

Mrs Gardiner threw a quick glance at her nieces and said smoothly, "That is most kind, Mr Darcy. I think I speak for my nieces when I say we should be glad to accept."

.

CHAPTER THREE

Elizabeth found herself strangely excited by the prospect of their engagement at Darcy House, and she saw that she was not the only one. A study of Jane's preoccupied air told her that her sister was also thinking of the invitation and the prospect of seeing Bingley again. It was not until they were in their shared bedchamber that evening, however, that Elizabeth found the chance to ask Jane about her feelings.

"I know I appeared discomfited for a moment in the parlour this morning," said Jane. "But 'twas merely a momentary sensation. I do assure you, I am not greatly perturbed by the prospect of seeing Mr Bingley again. He shall certainly remain as one of the most amiable gentleman of my acquaintance—but given his quick departure from Netherfield and his continued absence, I believe that I may have misinterpreted his intentions towards me during his stay in Hertfordshire. I am resolved not to make the same mistake again."

"We do not know the reason that he left Netherfield so swiftly," Elizabeth pointed out. "There may have been a perfectly legitimate reason why he was unable to return to the country. And you will admit that he could not send you a letter to explain himself, due to the dictates of society which prevents a gentleman from writing to a lady."

"Yes," said Jane quietly. "But he must have known that I was in town this past week, for I wrote to Miss Bingley as soon as we arrived. Surely she would have passed the news on to him? Therefore, I must conclude that they are aware of me being in London, but have no desire to renew the acquaintance."

"His sister, perhaps," said Elizabeth. "But not Mr Bingley, I am sure. No one who has seen you together can doubt the strength of his affections."

"Oh, Lizzy!" Jane sighed. "Would that you are right! But I shall not allow myself to hope— that way leads to heartache and disappointment. I shall simply think of him as nothing more than an amiable young man whose company I enjoy. I look forward to a pleasant evening at Darcy House and Mr Bingley will be no more than yet another of the guests that we are to meet there."

Elizabeth wanted to argue but decided that perhaps it was best to leave things as they were. She too did not want to raise false hopes for Jane. She knew that her sister's spirits had been very low since Bingley had left Netherfield. Even coming to town had not done much to lift her spirits. That morning had been the first time she had seen some colour in Jane's cheeks and she did not doubt that it was due to agitation at the thought of seeing Bingley again.

As for herself, Elizabeth felt a lively curiosity for Darcy House and its inhabitants. Naturally, her anticipation was for meeting the sister and not the brother, she assured herself. Indeed, the prospect of spending an evening in Darcy's company filled her with dread and not pleasure! Nevertheless, her thoughts returned continually to the prospect and she found that she was looking forward to the soirée with much impatience.

The next evening, Elizabeth looked out of the window excitedly as the carriage circled Grosvenor Square and pulled up in front of the elegant facade of Darcy House. With its six-pane sash windows and fluted pilasters in perfect symmetry with the pedimented portico, it was one of the most majestic residences in the square. They alighted from the carriage and mounted the steps to enter the impressive foyer with its high ceiling and checked marble floors. The butler took their wraps and coats, then led them towards the drawing room, from which the sounds of conversation and laughter could be heard. Everyone stopped talking and looked up as they entered, then Bingley sprang to his feet.

"Miss Bennet!" He hurried forwards, his blue eyes bright with excitement, and caught hold of Jane's hands. "When Darcy told me that you were in town, I was absolutely delighted! It has been a very long time since I have had the pleasure of seeing you—indeed, we have not met since the twenty-sixth of November, when we were dancing together at the Netherfield ball."

Jane blushed and gave him a shy smile. "I had not thought to find your memory so exact, Mr Bingley," she said.

"But of course it is exact!" he said, still holding her hands. "I cannot recollect a happier time than the few months I spent in Hertfordshire with your company... er... that is to say..." he stammered, reddening as he realised what he had uttered. He dropped his hands and looked away.

Darcy had approached them by now with his

sister, as host and hostess, to welcome the new guests. Elizabeth looked at Georgiana with interest. Like her brother, she was tall, but unlike him, she had yet to enter fully into adulthood. Her figure was not yet that of a grown woman and her manner brought to mind an eager schoolgirl delighted to be let out of the classroom at last. Indeed, she reminded Elizabeth a little of herself at the same age. Georgiana was perhaps slightly more reserved, though this was probably more due to the austere presence of her brother at her side. Elizabeth reflected wryly that if *she* had grown up with an elder brother like Darcy as guardian—instead of her indulgent parents— she was likely to be a very different person! When Georgiana darted a quick look upwards and caught her eye, Elizabeth gave her a warm smile and was gratified to see the other girl return it instantly.

They joined the other guests at the sofas: Caroline Bingley, Mr and Mrs Hurst, a stout lady in a silk puce gown and bejewelled turban who was introduced as the Darcys' neighbour, Mrs St John, and finally her distant cousin, Amy St John. The latter was a slight, mousy girl with light brown hair and a pale, freckled face. Her gown was distinctly plain and dowdy, and she looked embarrassed and uncomfortable in the company of such finery as worn by Caroline Bingley and Mrs Hurst, and even the expensive simplicity of Georgiana's attire. Elizabeth's own gown and that of Jane and her aunt were not as fashionable as those worn by the Bingley sisters, but they were elegant enough to pass muster. Elizabeth felt a wave of sympathy for Amy. She understood what it was like to live with meagre means.

Bingley's sisters made a great show of exclaiming their delight at seeing Jane again, though Caroline Bingley looked slightly embarrassed when Jane mentioned her letter.

"What? Have you been in town all this time?" interjected Bingley, looking indignant. "Why did nobody inform me?" He turned accusing eyes on his sister.

Caroline Bingley's cheeks reddened and she said awkwardly, "Your letter must have been waylaid somehow, for I do not believe I have received it. Had I known that you were in town, I would surely have called upon you."

Jane was satisfied with this response but Elizabeth was far more cynical. She was sure that behind the simpering smiles, the Bingley sisters had no real love for Jane and certainly no desire to see her as a member of their family. They would do everything in their power to prevent their brother from marrying a girl with such a lowly social position and poor connections. In fact, as Elizabeth observed the way Caroline Bingley kept glancing across at Darcy, she could see that they would infinitely prefer a union between Bingley and Georgiana, for this would bring the two families even closer. And—from Caroline Bingley's point of view—throw her into Darcy's path more frequently.

Nevertheless, it was clear for anyone to see that there was no special affection between Bingley and Georgiana. He treated her like a younger sister and she looked up to him as no more than a dear family friend. Indeed, now that Jane had arrived, Bingley's sole attention was devoted to the latter. He sat beside her and said little to anyone else, much to his sisters' annoyance.

Mrs Gardiner had entered easily into conversation with Mrs St John, and Mr Gardiner was conversing with Darcy and Mr Hurst about the finer points of trout fishing. With Jane and Bingley engrossed with each other, this left Elizabeth with no choice but to join the group comprised of Georgiana, Amy St John, and the two Bingley sisters. She was soon vexed to find that Caroline Bingley appeared to take great pleasure in teasing Amy—toying with her as a cat would with a mouse and deriving great amusement from the girl's discomfiture. She teased Amy mercilessly about her dowdy gown, her country complexion, and her humble position as the daughter of a poor clergyman.

Poor Amy was too timid to make more than stammering responses to Miss Bingley's remarks and spent a lot of her time flushed with embarrassment. Elizabeth longed to help her and had to bite her tongue several times to stop herself from uttering a retort in Amy's defence. She was gratified, however, to see that several others in the party had overheard Caroline's sneering comments. Georgiana spoke up several times in indignation for her friend and even Darcy sent Miss Bingley frowning looks.

CHAPTER FOUR

After a light supper, they reconvened in the drawing room, which connected to the music room, and the ladies were invited to display their talents at the pianoforte. Mrs Hurst immediately volunteered. An accomplished musician, she was proud of her skill at the keyboard and not bashful about showing off her abilities. Once she had played a few concertos, she invited her sister to come and accompany her in an aria. Caroline Bingley stood up with great aplomb and crossed the room in a slow, sauntering manner, clearly hoping to have everyone's eyes upon her. She struck a pose beside the pianoforte and, as the music started, she began to sing. She had a good voice—strong and throaty—and Elizabeth had to grudgingly admit that she and her sister made a fine pair. They finished to loud applause and Caroline Bingley smiled complacently.

"I wish I could sing like that..." Amy spoke up from where she was sitting on the sofa next to Elizabeth. She sighed wistfully. "But my voice is dreadfully thin and weak. Even if I had been able to afford lessons, I do not think any music tutor would have taken me on as a pupil."

"Oh, surely it is not as bad as that," said Elizabeth with an encouraging smile. "I am not blessed with an enviable voice either, though I have been taught the best way to project and enhance it. I am sure if you had the right tuition, you could improve greatly and enable your voice to fulfil its potential."

Amy gave her a shy smile. "Why, thank you, Miss Bennett. It is very kind of you to say that."

Elizabeth would have said more, but at that moment they were interrupted by Caroline Bingley's voice calling out to Georgiana to take her turn at the pianoforte. Darcy's sister rose obediently and made her way to the piano stool.

Caroline turned to Amy. "And what about you, Miss St John? I am sure we would all be delighted to hear your dulcet tones. Pray do indulge us with a song. It would be charming to see you accompany Miss Darcy on the instrument."

"N-n-no..." stammered Amy, her face going white. "Please... I beg you... I do not have the talent to sing—"

"Nonsense! We are all amongst friends here. You do not need to display such modesty," said Caroline with a malicious smile.

The other unsuspecting guests began to join in the urging, calling out and encouraging Amy to stand up and sing. Elizabeth saw the other girl's hands clench hard on the sofa cushion until her knuckles showed white. At last, with no choice, she stood up, trembling, and made her way to the side of the pianoforte. Georgiana gave her a sympathetic look, but Amy was hardly even looking at her friend. She was leaning against the pianoforte for support, her face drained of all colour and her eyes desperate. Elizabeth's heart went out to the terrified girl and she wondered if she should say something. However, she did not want to call more attention to the girl's failings and she also did not want to embarrass their hosts by causing a scene.

The music began and Amy gulped, then took a deep breath and began to sing. A thin, reedy voice filled the air. Elizabeth winced. The girl had not exaggerated: her voice was decidedly unmelodious and, now combined with a quavering quality from her nervousness, it was awful to listen to.

Elizabeth hesitated and was just agonising over whether to do something when, to her surprise, Darcy sprang up from his chair. She thought at first that he would turn and quit the room in disdain, as she had seen him do at the Netherfield ball when her sister, Mary, had made an embarrassing exhibition of herself on the pianoforte. But to her enormous surprise, Darcy strode across the room to join Amy beside the instrument.

He turned and directed a smile at the audience. "I find that I am suddenly seized with the urge to sing too," he said. He glanced at Amy. "Pray, Miss St John, would you do me the honour of allowing me to accompany you in a duet?"

"I-I... yes... I..." Amy stammered.

Darcy looked over the girl's head at his sister and gave a significant nod. Georgiana quickly switched to playing a different tune. Before anyone else could react, Darcy began to sing. He had a deep, rich baritone that filled the room and everybody smiled at the unexpected pleasure of seeing Darcy thus exert himself.

Elizabeth saw Amy's shaking slowly subside as she also began to sing softly next to him. His strong voice drowned out her weak one and the applause when they finished was sincere and enthusiastic.

"Bravo!"

"Delightful!"

"Darcy, man, I never knew you could sing so well."

Caroline Bingley flushed angrily as Amy made a curtsy and quickly sat down again. Elizabeth watched Darcy as he returned to his seat. It had been an uncommonly chivalrous thing for him to do and not what she had expected from him at all. It made her view him in a new light. She had not thought Darcy had it in him to be kind and generous, particularly to those beneath him in wealth and consequence—and yet tonight he had shown compassion for a poor country nobody and exerted himself greatly to do so.

Could she have been wrong about him?

Elizabeth was called for her turn on the pianoforte and she rose and went to the instrument. While she did not possess Mrs Hurst's skill or technical precision, she played with an easy, unaffected confidence which made her a pleasure to listen to and the applause for her, when she finished, was no less appreciative. She was aware of Darcy watching her intently from across the room and she was puzzled once again by his interest. But she ignored it as best she could and rejoined the others in the drawing room.

Thankfully, Caroline Bingley seemed to have abandoned her game of bullying Amy St John. Tea was served and everyone helped themselves, then broke up into small groups, as they settled once more on the various sofas and settees in the drawing room. Elizabeth carried her cup from the sideboard and hesitated, wondering which group to join. Her aunt was engrossed in conversation with Mrs St John and Elizabeth felt uncomfortable disturbing them. Mr and Mrs Hurst, Bingley and Jane had formed a set for cards, with her uncle looking on, and Elizabeth had no particular wish to join them either. She glanced across the room and smiled in amusement: Caroline Bingley was engaged in trying to flirt with Darcy. He remained coolly unresponsive, but Elizabeth knew that she would not be a welcome addition to *that* party. Finally, she spied Amy and Georgiana by the pianoforte and decided that she would enjoy their company. The two girls looked much more relaxed now that the music exhibition was over and were huddled together, giggling, as they looked down at something amongst the sheet music.

"May I join you?" Elizabeth asked as she approached them.

They both jumped and looked up, flushing

guiltily. Georgiana hastily pushed something beneath a sheet of music. Elizabeth was reminded of herself and her friend, Charlotte Lucas, in their younger years when they had shared secrets just like this. She remembered a time when they had been caught passing notes in church and had been severely reprimanded—particularly when it was discovered that the notes contained several unflattering drawings of Charlotte's strict governess.

Seeing the way Georgiana's eyes darted guiltily to Caroline Bingley now, Elizabeth wondered if the girls had been taking a similar form of revenge on the unpleasant woman. She could not really blame them—she was ashamed of a childish urge herself to want to draw Caroline Bingley with a large moustache!

She wisely kept such thoughts to herself, however, and happily embarked on a discussion of their favourite styles of music—though she was aware of Darcy's dark gaze on her the whole time and could not help wondering what that gentleman was thinking of her.

CHAPTER FIVE

Elizabeth was still mulling over Darcy's behaviour the next day as she sat in her aunt's parlour and attempted to read her book. But once again, she found her mind wandering constantly to one tall, handsome gentleman who both vexed and intrigued her. She was glad of the interruption when her aunt came into the parlour, holding the morning post.

"There is a letter here for you, Lizzy. I believe it is from Longbourn."

Jane looked up eagerly as Elizabeth took the letter from her aunt and broke the seal. It was from her youngest sister and was written in a hurried hand with blotches of ink all over the paper, as was Lydia's usual style.

"What does she say?" asked Jane.

Elizabeth scanned the page. "Oh... She is

greatly vexed that the officers will soon be leaving Meryton to encamp in Brighton for the summer... she is hoping that Papa might be persuaded to take us all there to stay... Heaven forbid!" Elizabeth looked up and grimaced at Jane. "Kitty and Lydia have been bad enough with one small regiment of the militia in Meryton. I shudder to think how they would conduct themselves in a whole camp full of soldiers. I hope Papa remains resistant to their schemes."

"Aye," Jane agreed. "It would be a most inopportune arrangement."

Elizabeth continued scanning the missive. "There has been some gossip relating to Mr Wickham. It appears that he is soon to be engaged to Mary King."

"Indeed?" Jane said in surprise. "But there did not seem to be much affection between them when we saw them at balls back in Meryton."

Elizabeth nodded, her eyes going back to the letter. "Yes, Lydia seems surprised as well. She claims that Wickham never cared for Mary King at all."

"Has Miss King not come into a sudden inheritance? Remember that Mrs Needham told us that she is now an heiress with ten thousand pounds," said Mrs Gardiner with a dry smile. "I would imagine that such a fortune would be the chief reason why Mr Wickham is now rendering himself agreeable to her."

"Oh, Wickham is not like that," said Elizabeth quickly.

"But he paid her not the smallest attention until her grandfather's death made her the beneficiary of this fortune," Mrs Gardiner pointed out.

"Well, why should he? You had previously warned me against an involvement with him due to the imprudence of such a match. But if it was not allowable for him to gain my affections because I had no money, what occasion could there be for making love to a girl he did not care about, and who was equally poor?" Elizabeth said impatiently. "I do not quarrel with him for his wish of independence. On the contrary, nothing could be more natural. I understand that handsome young men must have something to live on as well as the plain."

"Perhaps," her aunt agreed. "However, there seems indelicacy in directing his attentions towards Miss King, so soon after this event."

"A man in distressed circumstances has no time for that elegant decorum which other people may observe. If *she* does not object to it, why should *we*?"

"*Her* not objecting does not justify *him*. It may only show her being deficient in something herself—such as sense." Mrs Gardiner frowned. "Have care, Lizzy, for your bias in Wickham's favour may lead you to blind prejudice in that arena."

Elizabeth opened her mouth to retort, then shut it again. Her aunt's remonstration made her uncomfortable. Was she guilty of prejudice? It was true that she had found Wickham's flirtatious manners and easy charm most entertaining. His attentions to her had been extremely flattering—though she had to admit that she was not truly upset by this news of his engagement. Yes, she had thought him the most agreeable man she had ever met and had enjoyed the thought of a possible attachment. But now that this possibility was over, she found that her heart had been but slightly touched, and her vanity was satisfied with believing that *she* could have been his choice, had his situation permitted it.

Nevertheless, Elizabeth had to admit that she did harbour a partiality where Wickham was concerned. Was she prone to accepting his words far more readily than an account from someone like Darcy, because Wickham had flattered her whereas the latter had wounded her pride in snubbing her? Feeling uncomfortable about these revelations of her own character, Elizabeth attempted to change the subject.

"Is there any other interesting post?"

Mrs Gardner rifled through the rest of the pile then paused, pulling out a gilt-edged card. "Oh my word... yes! Here is an invitation to Lady Grantley's charity ball tomorrow evening. I certainly would not have expected to be on her guest list. However, I recall Mr Darcy and Mr Bingley speaking of this event last night and asking me if we were to attend. I wonder if they are behind this last-minute invitation. I know that Lady Grantley is an old family friend of the Darcys. It is certainly a great honour. These are not circles your uncle and I are used to moving in." She looked at Jane and smiled. "I have a feeling that Bingley may have had a hand in this. There is no doubt that he is keen for any opportunity to see you again."

Jane blushed prettily.

"How fortunate that we did all that shopping yesterday," added Mrs Gardiner with satisfaction. "Your new blue gown is perfect for the ball, Jane, and you will look delightful in it."

Lady Grantley's home was one of the most majestic residences in Regent's Park and Elizabeth, Jane, and the Gardiners looked around in admiration as they entered the ballroom. It was opulently decorated with gold gilding along the full-length mirrors which lined one wall of the room and magnificent chandeliers looming from the ceilings. An orchestra played at one end of the ballroom and chairs were arranged around the sides for those who were not partaking in the dancing. Crowds of people milled about the ballroom, all dressed in the height of fashion, with the gentlemen in perfectly tailored evening dress and the ladies sporting elaborate hairstyles and glittering jewels.

They had barely been there a few minutes before Bingley hurried to their side and carried Jane off for the first dance. Elizabeth could not hide a smile at the gentleman's eagerness—it seemed as if Bingley had been spending his time just waiting for Jane to appear! It was lovely to see how ardent his attentions were and how radiant Jane looked in the glow of his affection. There were several smiling glances as people watched them dance and Elizabeth could see many admiring Jane's beauty. She was just turning to share the observation with her aunt when she felt a light hand on her elbow.

"Miss Bennet... fancy meeting you here!"

Elizabeth turned to see a pretty girl with red hair and a lightly freckled face. "Why, Miss King! I had not realised that you were in London."

The other girl grimaced. "My uncle insisted that I come to town with him. I was most put out for I was having a capital time in Meryton. We had several parties after you left, Miss Bennet! 'Tis a shame you had to miss them. Your sisters have been enjoying themselves immensely."

"I'm sure they have," Elizabeth said with a wry smile.

"Yes, and we have all been most dismayed at the thought of the regiment leaving us!" Mary King continued. "Oh, what shall we do without the delightful company of the officers?" She paused and gave Elizabeth a coy little smile. "I own, though, that I shall not suffer as much... for I am fortunate to have gained the particular affection of a certain officer named Wickham."

"Yes, I... er... had heard that you and he have reached a special understanding?" Elizabeth said delicately.

Mary King's smile deepened. "Oh, it is not official yet. Darling Wickham has not had a chance to speak to my uncle yet and gain his consent... but he assured me when we parted that he would follow me to London directly. I hope he may be in town by tomorrow." She giggled. "I am sure it will not be long before I shall be walking down the aisle at his side."

"I wish you every happiness," said Elizabeth.

"Thank you." The other girl clasped

Elizabeth's hand. "Oh, I do hope we shall meet often while I am in town. I shall not feel so alone here if I am able to see some of my acquaintances from Meryton."

They were interrupted at this moment by two young men soliciting their hands for the next dance and Elizabeth's attention was soon engaged by a string of partners eager to claim her. She enjoyed dancing and normally partook of the activity with great enthusiasm and full dedication. Tonight, however, she found herself slightly distracted. As she moved down the set, she kept looking around the ballroom and feeling slightly deflated when she could see no sign of one tall, dark figure. Was Darcy not attending the ball? She would have thought that he would have come to escort his sister. Until this moment, she had not realised how much she had been expecting to see him.

Not that I wish to see him, Elizabeth corrected herself hastily. *It is merely strange to see Bingley without him.*

As she glanced around the room once again, she caught sight of another familiar figure: Amy St John was sitting by herself on one of the chairs along the wall, looking very small and lost in the crowd. Elizabeth observed her over the next few dances and could see that no one approached the girl to ask her to dance. Amy seemed to shrink even more as she continued to be ignored. Mrs St John sat nearby, but was too busily engaged in conversation with a few other matrons to notice her young cousin's distress. Elizabeth felt a stab of pity for the girl and, when she had finished the dance, excused herself and made her way over to Amy's side.

CHAPTER SIX

"Oh, Miss Bennet!" Amy looked up in relief as she saw Elizabeth. "It is so wonderful to see someone I know."

Elizabeth sat down next to her with a smile. "Yes, these balls can be a bit daunting, can't they? Arriving amongst strangers and not knowing anyone to strike up conversation with."

"That does not seem to be a problem for you," observed Amy shyly. "You seem to have a wonderful talent for conversing easily with anybody you encounter."

Elizabeth laughed. "That is a polite way of saying that I am far too forward and bold with my opinions."

"Oh, no, indeed not! I am full of admiration for your confidence and independent spirit," said Amy. "I wish I had a tiny measure of your self-aplomb." She looked down sadly. "Indeed, I do not feel that I even ought to be here, dressed as I am…"

Elizabeth followed her gaze and winced slightly. She had to admit that the girl had a point. Amy's simple gown of faded yellow muslin looked plain and dowdy amongst all the finery in the room, and her thin brown hair was pulled back in a severe knot which did nothing to enhance her features. She racked her brains for something to say that would be kind yet honest, but before she could say anything, they were startled by a deep voice saying next to them:

"You must not let other people's attitudes weigh with you, Miss St John. Pomp and finery are not everything."

They turned to see Darcy standing beside them, with Georgiana next to him. Elizabeth felt her pulse give a little jump. It was simply from being startled to find him suddenly next to her, she assured herself. She noticed, however, that Darcy was not looking at her. His eyes were on Amy instead, his gaze soft and kind. Georgiana hurriedly sat down next to her friend and apologised for their tardiness.

"Oh, please forgive me, Amy! I did not like to leave you alone for so long," said Georgiana. "We were delayed as my brother had a matter of business he had to see to and he returned late from his club."

"'Tis of no consequence. Miss Bennet has been most kind and kept me company," said Amy with a shy smile at Elizabeth.

"Mr Darcy! Georgiana!"

They turned to see Caroline Bingley rushing up to them.

"Why, I had almost given you up for lost! Where have you been?" Miss Bingley gave Darcy a flirtatious look. "I declare, Mr Darcy, no ball is complete without your noble presence."

"You flatter me, madam."

She glanced at the dance floor, then back at Darcy. "And might we see you dance, sir? I know you do not often indulge in the activity—though you cut such a fine figure when you do!"

"You know I do not normally care to dance, Miss Bingley," said Darcy.

"Oh, I completely understand, Mr Darcy!" gushed Caroline Bingley. "There is nothing as savage as some of those country dances we saw in Hertfordshire. However, here in London we are amongst more refined company and I know that you do grace the dance floor on occasion. Perhaps there is a young lady here tonight lucky enough to capture your fancy?" She raised her eyebrows and surreptitiously smoothed down her gown, showing her figure to advantage.

Darcy looked at her thoughtfully, then said, "Yes, I do believe that the choice of partner can turn a tedious activity into a pleasurable one."

The musicians struck up again and couples began forming a new set. Darcy gave a brief smile. "Very well, I shall dance tonight—and I may join this set now."

He turned to the young ladies assembled before him. Elizabeth saw Caroline Bingley lean forwards, an expectant expression on her face. She herself was suddenly reminded of Darcy's application for her hand for the dance at the Netherfield ball and wondered if he would ask her again. She was just thinking of how to answer him when, to everybody's surprise, Darcy stepped forwards and bowed to Amy.

"Miss St John—would you do me the honour of standing up with me for this dance?"

Amy stared at him, speechless. Caroline made a choking sound. Darcy ignored her and led the young country girl onto the dance floor whilst Georgiana smiled in delight. Elizabeth sat down in the chair that Amy had vacated and watched them as they joined the other couples and began to move down the set. For someone who professed to dislike the activity, Darcy was an excellent dancer. He moved with a commanding grace and consummate skill, leading Amy gently through the set, guiding her expertly and shielding her from the clumsiness of the other dancers.

Elizabeth was aware of an uncomfortable feeling in her breast and she was surprised after a moment to realise that it felt very much like jealousy! *Surely I am not jealous of Amy for gaining Mr Darcy's attentions?* And yet she had to admit that she *had* expected Darcy to ask *her* to dance—she had been smugly sure of it— and had even been planning to give him a witty refusal. It had been a provoking to realise that she was not his choice.

Furthermore, she could see that Darcy's actions were not going unnoticed. All around the room, there were nods and whispers as people watched him dancing with Amy St John and began to speculate.

"*Who is that girl? Clergyman's daughter did you say? Why is Fitzwilliam Darcy paying her so much attention? Oh my dear... that gown... but still, there must be something about her if Darcy is choosing to dance with her—you know what a high stickler he is! Perhaps he has developed a* tendre *for the girl?*"

Elizabeth turned to Georgiana next to her. "Your brother is an excellent dancer."

"Yes, he is, though he would never admit to it." The girl grinned at Elizabeth. "When I was taking dance lessons, Fitzwilliam would always come and volunteer his services as my partner. It was very good of him, for I imagine the hours of practice must have been very tedious." She looked at Darcy and Amy once more. "It is very kind of him to ask Amy to dance; it was her greatest fear, you know, that she should remain a wallflower."

"Yes, that is a fate that all young ladies dread," Elizabeth agreed. "But perhaps now that your brother has led the way, other young men will follow suit."

"Oh, I hope so," Georgiana said fervently. "Then they would have a chance to acquaint themselves with Amy better and realise what a delightful creature she is!" She turned wide eyes on Elizabeth. "Oh, Miss Bennet, how wonderful it would be if Amy were to receive a proposal of marriage. Then she would no longer have to worry about working in a seminary. She could live in comfort and security."

"Yes," Elizabeth said, although with Amy's plain looks and lack of fortune, she thought the chances of an eligible match were very slim. However, she kept her thoughts to herself, not wanting to dampen Georgiana's enthusiasm.

The other girl sighed wistfully. "But first we must find someone for Amy to fall in love with—and for him to love her back..."

Elizabeth looked at her in amusement, feeling suddenly much older than her twenty-one years. "Most marriages in society are not based on love, you know," she said gently.

"Oh, I know," Georgiana's face darkened. "And I think it is abominable! How can you pledge to spend the rest of your life with someone if you do not love him passionately? No, I could never contemplate marriage without love."

Though Elizabeth shared the girl's abhorrence of a marriage with no respect or genuine affection, she could not help a more cynical view of matters. With Georgiana's fortune of thirty-thousand pounds and her position as a member of one of the most powerful families in England, Darcy's sister would not have to worry about sacrificing her better feelings for material comfort. But Elizabeth knew that love was not a luxury that those in less fortunate circumstances could always afford. For one such as Amy, she would be lucky if she were to receive an offer from at least one decent, kind man who could give her a comfortable home. Still, Elizabeth held her tongue once again, not wanting to taint Georgiana's youthful idealism with her own cynicism.

"If only Amy had some prettier gowns to

wear..." Georgiana fretted. "And her hair could be arranged so much better! Miss Bennet, I have some gowns which have been little-used and Amy and I are about the same size. Do you think she would be offended if I were to offer her some gowns for her use and suggested a change of hairstyle?"

"I think you know her far better than I," said Elizabeth cautiously. "But I would imagine that Miss St John would be extremely grateful for your generosity and suggestions."

"Yes, I hope so!" said Georgiana enthusiastically. "And perhaps I will ask Fitzwilliam to escort her to a few events with us—people always pay attention whenever he is around. If he demonstrates kindness towards Amy, everybody else will too."

Georgiana's words seemed prophetic, for when Darcy returned Amy to her seat at last, he was quickly followed by a number of young men who suddenly seemed anxious to make her acquaintance. Now that a man of Darcy's consequence had shown Amy attention, many others were keen to follow his example. The girl was soon surrounded by several suitors vying for her attention and her face flushed with rosy colour, making her look almost pretty. A few moments later, she was led back onto the dance floor by Lord Denning, the young Earl of Shrewsbury, whilst Georgiana watched, beaming.

By the end of the evening, Amy had been asked for dance after dance and was almost as popular as many of the wealthy young ladies in the room. Elizabeth could see from her happy smiles and sparkling eyes that Amy was enjoying a ball for the first time, and again she felt a flicker of gratitude to Darcy for his kindness towards the girl.

But was it just kindness? Elizabeth mused as she watched Darcy standing next to his sister and her friend. He had not danced again with anyone else in the room and this had not gone unremarked. Naturally, his attentive behaviour could be explained as nothing more than gallantry towards his sister's friend, but there were many who were beginning to wonder if Darcy had designs on the girl himself.

Elizabeth had been vexed to find herself amongst those who watched Darcy avidly, wondering if he might ask anyone else to dance. Surely she was not hoping he might ask her? No, no, she was certainly not hoping for his attentions. And if it was true that Darcy had formed an attachment for Amy St John, she would pity the girl. Imagine capturing the attention of such a proud, disagreeable man!

Nevertheless, as they finally took their leave at the end of the evening, Elizabeth was conscious of a deep sense of disappointment that the proud, disagreeable man had never asked her to dance.

CHAPTER SEVEN

Darcy was not especially pleased when he came down to breakfast the following morning to find that Bingley and his sisters had called early at Darcy House and were already at the table with Georgiana. In truth, he did not mind Bingley's company, but he could have done without the gentleman's sisters. He had been hoping for a quiet meal where he could read the morning paper and eat his breakfast in peace, but he had barely sat down at the table before Caroline Bingley began to speak of the previous night and ask his opinion on the ball.

"Louisa and I were quite surprised by your gallant championing of Miss St John, Mr Darcy," said Miss Bingley archly. "I declare, it was most kind of you to give attention to such a dowdy little nobody."

Georgiana looked up indignantly. "Amy isn't

a nobody!" she said. "She is my great friend."

Caroline Bingley smiled. "Oh, I suppose that would explain your brother taking pity on her plight last night."

Darcy spoke up, "I was not moved merely by pity."

Miss Bingley looked at him quickly. When he did not elaborate, she gave a nervous laugh. "Why, Mr Darcy—are you saying that you have formed an attachment to the girl?"

Darcy gave her a level look. "If I had, it would be my private affair."

Caroline Bingley gave another nervous laugh and attempted a teasing tone. "You do seem to have quite a penchant for homely country girls, do you not, sir? I remember when we were in Hertfordshire, you seemed quite taken with Miss Eliza Bennet and her 'fine eyes'."

Darcy made no response to this and Miss Bingley bit her lip in frustration.

"Speaking of Miss Bennet..." she continued desperately. "I was surprised at how very ill she looked last night. I never in my life saw anyone so much altered since I last saw her." She glanced at Mrs Hurst for support. "Louisa and I were agreeing that we should not have known her again."

Mrs Hurst nodded. "Indeed. Most shocking."

Georgiana looked up indignantly again. "I think Miss Bennet is very pretty," she said.

"Well... I must confess, I never could see any beauty in her," Caroline continued, her eyes on Darcy, still hoping to get a reaction out of him. "I remember, when we were first in Hertfordshire, how amazed we all were to find that she was a reputed beauty."

"I thought Elizabeth Bennet looked very well," Bingley protested. "And her sister too."

Darcy gave his friend a wry look and refrained from saying that Bingley was likely to think Jane Bennet would look well if she had turned up to the ball in a gunny sack! Nevertheless, he was forced to concede that the eldest Miss Bennet had indeed looked lovely the night before—clad in a light blue gown which set off her fair complexion and brought out the blue in her eyes.

It was the second Miss Bennet, however, who had really caught his admiration. Though he had done his best to ignore her all evening and had resisted the impulse to ask her to dance, he had been aware of Elizabeth the whole time—her every move, every smile, every gesture. And in spite of Caroline's claims to the contrary, Darcy thought Elizabeth had looked radiant in a soft peach gown trimmed with satin ribbons and her dark brown hair caught up in an elegant topknot. She had not boasted the lavish jewels that many of the other ladies at the ball had worn, but to Darcy, she had little need for such embellishments, for she had seemed to glow with beauty from within...

What am I thinking?

Darcy took a sip of coffee, impatient with himself for these fanciful thoughts. Although he had given in to impulse the other day and used the misplaced parcels as a pretext to see Elizabeth again—and then continued indulging his weakness by inviting her to their soirée—he had since been forcing himself to put her from his mind. It was something he was still wrestling with, but he had believed that his wayward thoughts were under good regulation. Until now.

Darcy became aware that Caroline Bingley was still awaiting his response. Perhaps if he answered her at last, she might drop the subject and leave him in peace.

He looked at her and said coolly, "I am not aware of any great change in either Miss Bennett but I have to confess that I was not particularly looking."

For a moment, Caroline Bingley looked uncertain as to whether she liked this answer, then, to Darcy's relief, she seemed to decide that she was satisfied and turned her attention back to her breakfast.

"I do have an excessive regard for Jane Bennett—she is really a very sweet girl," said Mrs Hurst magnanimously. "'Tis a pity that she is so poorly settled. With such a family and such low connections, I'm afraid she will have very little chance of making a good marriage."

Bingley looked up, his brow furrowing. "I—"

"Yes, and you do know that their aunt and uncle, who were with them at the ball last night, reside in Cheapside?" said Caroline Bingley in tones of mock horror.

"Oh? Perhaps we ought to call upon them when we next have an opportunity?" said Mrs Hurst with a sneer and both women laughed uproariously.

"If they had uncles enough to fill all Cheapside, it would not make them less agreeable to me," cried Bingley.

"But it must very materially lessen the chance of them marrying men of any consideration in the world," said Darcy, suddenly joining in the conversation. "These things cannot be ignored. Social position and consequence are important qualities in selecting a bride, in the times we live in."

Georgiana looked at her brother in disappointment. "Oh, Fitzwilliam—surely those qualities are less important than love?"

"I agree. Such attributes would not matter a jot to me," said Bingley firmly.

Caroline Bingley looked at him in surprise. "Charles—you are not serious? Are you saying that you have formed a definite attachment to

Jane Bennett?"

"You would do well to put such ideas from your head, Bingley," said Darcy curtly. "It would save you from the inconvenience of a most imprudent marriage."

"Yes indeed!" cried his sister. "I cannot believe that you even entertained the notion, Charles!"

Bingley jutted his chin out. "I think Jane Bennett is the most wonderful, beautiful, lovely creature I have ever met—"

"Yes, she is lovely," said Darcy impatiently. "But what of her relations? What of her circumstances? What of her social position and her connections? You would be ill advised to choose such a marriage partner."

Bingley opened his mouth to argue, then shut it again and sat back, the expression on his face mutinous. Georgiana gave his arm a sympathetic squeeze. Darcy returned his attention to his plate and attempted to continue eating. He should have been congratulating himself on successfully convincing his friend of the folly of his actions. Instead, he discovered that he felt uneasy. He had suddenly realised that the vehemence of his arguments against Jane Bennett had less to do with genuine concern for Bingley's welfare and more to do with his own! The arguments he had put forth were very much what he kept telling himself when his thoughts turned towards considering Elizabeth Bennet as his bride.

Propose to Elizabeth? I must be mad!

And yet that was exactly what his heart had been whispering to him these past few days. Since seeing her again in London, his feelings for her had only grown. She filled his thoughts in the day and tormented his dreams at night. There was no other woman who had captivated him so. There was a mixture of playfulness and sweetness in Elizabeth's manner that completely entranced him.

She was the first woman who seemed unimpressed by his wealth and consequence. Consequently, he knew not how to deal with her. Unlike all the other woman who fawned over him, Elizabeth Bennet paid him little regard and he was at a loss how to approach her. He thought back to the ball the previous night and how much he had wanted to ask her to dance again—but his pride had shied away from the possibility of her giving him another public rejection, as she had when she had playfully refused to dance with him at the Lucases' party back in Hertfordshire.

In any case, it is for the best, Darcy told himself savagely. As he had advised Bingley, it was a union of the most imprudent kind and he should not have even be considering it. For his duty to family honour and to his name, he could not justify it.

And yet, as he glanced at Bingley once more and saw his friend's agonised expression, Darcy felt a sudden wish to confess to Bingley that he knew exactly what he was going through.

CHAPTER EIGHT

Elizabeth was surprised the following morning when two unexpected visitors were shown into the Gardiners' modest parlour. Georgiana Darcy and Amy St John had come to call and Elizabeth was very conscious of the great honour bestowed upon them—and by extension, on her aunt. She was gratified to think that Darcy's sister did not find the address of Cheapside too contemptible to visit and she wryly compared her civility to the Bingley sisters, who had noticeably made no gesture of social welcome.

"Miss Darcy! Miss St John! What a delightful surprise." Elizabeth rose to greet them. "My aunt and my sister, Jane, have just gone out for a moment—but they should return shortly. May I offer you tea?"

The bell was rung for refreshments and the ladies sat down together. Georgiana turned to Elizabeth eagerly.

"Miss Bennet, I had to call upon you as I was most excited to share my news. Amy has agreed to allow me to help her with her transformation!"

Elizabeth looked at the other girl who blushed and smiled shyly. "Indeed, I am very grateful that Miss Darcy should be spending so much time and effort on me."

"Oh, 'tis no bother at all. It shall be capital fun," said Georgiana delightedly. "I cannot wait to start. I have already asked my maid to alter a few of my gowns to suit Amy's figure and I shall have Monsieur Picard, the renowned hairdresser, come and advise us on how to style Amy's hair... oh, I cannot wait to see what she will look like!"

Amy blushed even more and looked almost uncomfortable to have so much attention centred on her.

"I shall look forward to seeing this transformation," said Elizabeth with a smile.

"You shall make your debut at Bingley's dinner party," said Georgiana grandly. "It will not be a large affair but there will be enough people there to admire your new look, including..." She gave her friend a mischievous look. "...several of the young men who were at

Lady Grantley's ball."

The other girl shifted uncomfortably. "Oh, do you think that advisable? Mr Bingley's sisters are such women of high fashion and disdainful tastes... I confess that they intimidate me greatly. I should not like to put myself forward and catch their notice. Perhaps we should wait until another event—"

"Oh, nonsense," said Georgiana. "I do not care a fig for Caroline Bingley's opinion! And you should not either, Amy. She is most unkind sometimes and I do not think her approval worth seeking. My brother thinks highly of you and his opinion is much more worthy."

Elizabeth looked at Georgiana quickly, but the other girl was chattering on, oblivious to the implication her words had suggested. She glanced at Amy St John and wondered again at the true reason for Darcy's attentions to the girl at Lady Grantley's ball.

Though Elizabeth was enjoying her stay in London, one of the things she missed were her long walks in the countryside. So she was delighted when Mrs Gardiner suggested a visit to Hyde Park. Though it would not be the same as a long country ramble—for they were to join the crowd promenading through the park during the "fashionable hour"—it would still be an opportunity to stretch her legs and enjoy some fresh air.

They arrived early at the park and Elizabeth breathed deeply and smiled as they entered through Queen Elizabeth's Gate at Hyde Park Corner. She drank in the sight of the picturesque trees, the flowering shrubs, and the wide green spaces stretching out around her. At around three hundred acres, Hyde Park was not the largest of the Royal Parks in London, but it was certainly one of the most popular and favoured by society. Looking at the happy alliance between the beautifully landscaped gardens at the south end of the park and the wilder, open meadows in the northern sections, Elizabeth could see why this green sanctuary was a favourite with so many.

"I do wish we could go to the north end of the park," she said with a sigh. "I long to *really* stretch my legs, to maybe even have a run across the meadows—"

"But, my dear, you can do that back in Hertfordshire at any time," Mrs Gardiner chided her gently. "One cannot come to London and not experience the spectacle of Rotten Row during the fashionable hour. Indeed, in the height of the season, it is 'the' place to be seen and attracts all that is wealthy, fashionable, and beautiful in London society. It is said that one might even catch a glimpse of Beau Brummell, or Georgiana the Duchess of Devonshire, or even the Prince Regent himself."

"I do not know if that would impress *me*," Elizabeth muttered.

"Surely—with your enjoyment of people-watching—you would appreciate such an occasion! It is a veritable show of the finest carriages and prime bloodstock, handled by the most fashionably dressed. Everyone is busy exchanging the latest gossip, meeting those of influence, maybe even engaging in a little discreet flirtation..." Mrs Gardiner gave a chuckle.

"*I* should like to see the fashionably dressed ladies and admire their riding habits and equipage, even if Lizzy isn't interested," said Jane with a smile.

"Oh, very well," Elizabeth grumbled. "Though I hope I shall not be run over by some young buck showing off his paces in his racing curricle."

"There is no fear of that," said Mrs Gardiner. "There are strict rules for the use of the Row and all riders and carriages are expected to maintain a sedate and decorous pace during the afternoon promenade."

"You mean, one is never allowed to gallop a horse here?"

"Only early in the mornings before

breakfast." Mrs Gardiner smiled. "In any case, there are footpaths alongside the Row separated from the main bridle path by wooden fencing, so you should be quite safe."

They had walked from the wrought iron gates by now and joined the long, wide bridle path—about eighty feet wide—known as Rotten Row. Elizabeth saw that her aunt was right. A steady procession of carriages and riders moved along the Row, whilst a large crowd of people matched their pace on the footpath alongside. There was a hum of excitement in the air and Elizabeth found herself caught up in the atmosphere.

They walked part of the way down the Row, then Mrs Gardiner—who had had a disturbed night due to one of her children being ill—decided that she was too fatigued to complete the entire walk. She decided to rest at a park bench on a grassy knoll beside the footpath, but urged her nieces to continue without her. They could retrieve her on their return and in the meantime she could enjoy the view from her stationary vantage point.

The two Bennet sisters continued on, enjoying the various sights. Elizabeth was just observing a passing barouche coach with interest—with its handsome matched footmen and spotted Dalmatian dogs—when she suddenly recognised the gentleman on horseback approaching them.

"Why, Mr Wickham!" she cried, smiling with pleasure at seeing the young officer.

His eyes lit up as he saw her as well and he took off his hat to give them a jaunty wave. When he had reached them, he reined in his horse and dismounted, then caught both their hands in his, bending over each to press a kiss on the backs of their fingers. Elizabeth laughed at his flamboyant behaviour, though she could see several older ladies in the carriages around them frowning at such forwardness

"We had not realised that you were in London, Mr Wickham," said Jane.

"It is but a brief visit," said Wickham.

"Have you come to be with Miss King?" asked Elizabeth. "I understand that congratulations are in order."

Wickham's face darkened slightly. "I am afraid you have been misinformed, Miss Bennet. I am not engaged to Miss King."

"Oh, I beg your pardon," said Elizabeth, embarrassed for him. "Perhaps it was a thoughtless indiscretion on my younger sister Lydia's part. I received news from her that you were to be married soon. And indeed, I met Miss King myself at a ball not two nights ago and she seemed to confirm that there was an understanding between you. "

"Oh, Miss King and I are of the same mind,"

said Wickham quickly. "There is nothing that would make her happier than to marry me. But alas, her uncle sees things differently." He scowled. "He does not look with compassion on my present circumstances. Indeed, he believes the worse of me and thinks me nothing more than a fortune hunter after Miss King's inheritance."

"But who could think such a thing?" said Jane, horrified. "That is most unkind and unwarranted. Are you sure there has not been some mistake—perhaps some misrepresentation that has led Miss King's uncle to think ill of you?"

Wickham laughed bitterly. "The only misrepresentation is my position as a soldier with no fortune, when I should have been a respectable man with a good living." He shook his head. "But alas, as you know, I was refused the rights to my legacy, though it was willed to me. Such has been my lot ever since the abuse I suffered at the hands of a certain gentleman."

Though he did not mention Darcy's name, Elizabeth had no doubt of whom he was referring to and her chest rose with indignation. She had already heard the story of Darcy's arrogant mistreatment of Wickham with horror and disbelief back in Meryton. To think that Darcy's arrogant interference was now robbing Wickham of the chance of a happy marriage! It was too much. The past few days had led her to think that she might have been wrong in her estimation of Darcy's character. In spending more time with him and observing some of his behaviour, she had hoped that she had mistaken Darcy—that perhaps he was a better man than she had thought.

Now she was conscious of the strong sense of disappointment. And Wickham's reminder of the injustice he had suffered due to Darcy's pride and conceit brought back all her old hostility towards the gentleman.

"It is most unjust!" said Elizabeth. "I wonder that you should let Darcy go unchallenged."

"Who am I to argue with the great Darcy?" said Wickham with a bitter smile. "The world is blinded by Darcy's fortune and consequence and easily swayed by his opinion."

Elizabeth recalled the way Darcy's behaviour to Amy had completely changed her status at the ball... and the way Georgiana had confided about her brother's influence. Wickham was right. He was no match for a man of such power. Darcy had a most unfair advantage!

Wickham's expression lightened and he grinned, looking at them with a return of his usual cheerful self. "Never fear. If I—"

He broke off and looked beyond them, his eyes widening. Elizabeth whirled around and saw a gentleman approaching them down the promenade.

Fitzwilliam Darcy.

CHAPTER NINE

Darcy was walking with his sister, Georgiana, on one arm, and her friend, Amy St John, on the other. The young country miss was looking up at Darcy and saying something to him, her face alight with laughter, and Elizabeth was struck by how pretty she looked at that moment. Darcy smiled down at her and Elizabeth was pricked by a sudden feeling of irritation.

They were walking in the thick of the throng and had not seen Wickham, Elizabeth, and Jane yet. It was not until Darcy and his companions were almost next to them that the crowd parted, and they were suddenly face-to-face. Darcy went very still, his eyes going flat and cold.

Wickham did not miss a beat. He swept one

of his flamboyant bows. "It is a pleasure to see you, Mr Darcy," he said smoothly. He turned towards Georgiana, who was looking at him hesitantly, and reached for her hand. "And I am delighted to see you again too, Miss Darcy."

Darcy stepped in front of Georgiana and glared at Wickham.

"Don't you *dare* address my sister!" he said through gritted teeth.

Putting a hand under Georgiana's elbow, he jerked her aside and urged her past. She threw a bewildered look back, her eyes on Wickham, then allowed herself to be led away. Amy hurried after them.

Several other people had also witnessed the exchange and noted Darcy's hostile reaction. There were raised eyebrows and whispers all around. Wickham, however, seemed remarkably unperturbed by the scene which had just occurred. He gave Elizabeth a sardonic smile and said with a shrug:

"You see? Mr Darcy continues his vendetta against me still."

"You are too good, Mr Wickham," cried Elizabeth. "I would not be able to stand such treatment! And all due to his abominable pride!" She shook her head. "I do remember of his boasting one day, at Netherfield, of the implacability of his resentments, of his having an unforgiving temper—"

"Lizzy..." Jane chided gently. "There may be extenuating circumstances unknown to us. Surely we ought not to judge Mr Darcy by a few words taken out of context—"

"I beg your pardon. I have seen enough of Mr Darcy to know that the context of those words is *most* appropriate in this case," retorted Elizabeth.

Wickham smiled. "Thank you, Miss Bennet for your defence of me. It is good to know that I still have some friends in this world who are not swayed merely by wealth and consequence."

"You have that in me," said Elizabeth firmly. "*I* do not fear Mr Darcy, nor do his power and social position hold much sway with me."

Wickham caught her hand again. "You do not know how much it means to me to hear that, Miss Bennet." He hesitated. "Indeed, I wondered if I might beg your assistance..."

"If I am able to help, I should certainly be glad to give it," said Elizabeth warmly.

Wickham reached into his coat's inner pocket and withdrew a folded note. "There is a letter I wish to deliver to Miss King, but her uncle has thwarted all my attempts to communicate with her. Could you conduct this note to her on my behalf?"

Elizabeth hesitated. "Sir, I..."

"I understand it is not entirely proper,"

Wickham said quickly. "Indeed, I would not ask were it not desperate. It is a note of goodbye, you see. I understand the reasons why we cannot be together but I do not want Miss King to think that I have simply abandoned her. I know she will pine and grieve should she have no explanation from my own lips. She may even continue to wait in hope—and I want to wish her well and urge her to forget me and continue with her life."

"That is a most laudable sentiment," said Jane, her eyes full of admiration.

"I love her," said Wickham. "And I simply wish her to be happy."

Elizabeth was very moved by Wickham's words and the expression of pain and humility in his countenance. She reached out and took the note.

"I shall do it for you," she promised. "Mr Bingley and his sister, Caroline, are hosting a dinner party jointly with the Hursts tomorrow evening. I am sure Miss King is invited so I shall see her then and be sure to pass on your letter."

"I am greatly indebted to you. Thank you," said Wickham, pressing another kiss to the back of her hand. "And now, I must bid you two ladies adieu. It has been a pleasure meeting you again. Please convey my regards to your parents."

Taking off his hat, he swept another bow, then mounted his horse once again and was gone down the path, out of sight.

"Heavens... we must return to our aunt!" said Jane. "Our pleasurable interlude with Mr Wickham has extended our walk far longer than we intended. She will be wondering where we are."

Elizabeth agreed and they turned back. As they walked, however, Elizabeth's thoughts returned to the recent encounter and she thought again with indignation of the unkindness that Wickham had suffered. Jane listened patiently as she gave vent to her feelings, but refused to accept the condemnation of Darcy's character. In her characteristic fashion, Jane strove to defend both young men and continue to think well of them.

"Oh, Jane, you cannot deny Mr Darcy's involvement in this regard!" Elizabeth said in frustration.

"I do not deny it. But I do not believe that he may be as bad as Mr Wickham says he is. There must be a mistake or a misunderstanding—indeed, I believe both may have been deceived. But it is impossible for us to conjecture the causes or circumstances which alienated them without knowing the details."

"We *have* the details," said Elizabeth stubbornly. "Wickham gave them to me in Meryton most assiduously: names, facts, everything mentioned without ceremony. The whole sorry account of his mistreatment at Darcy's hands: from old Mr Darcy's will and the bequest that was promised to him, to young Mr Darcy's refusal to honour the terms of the will and his despicable act of giving it away to another."

"Lizzy..." Jane scolded gently. "One cannot always rely on the veracity of a single account."

"Are you saying that Wickham is lying?"

Jane shifted uncomfortably. "No, indeed not! But perhaps he is unaware of his own misinformation. After all... do consider, Lizzy, what a disgraceful light this places Mr Darcy under. Would he really treat his father's favourite in such a manner, and one whom his father promised to provide for? And what of Mr Bingley? How can Mr Bingley be in friendship with Mr Darcy if the latter were to be such a man? How could they suit each other?"

"I could more easily believe Mr Bingley's being imposed on, than that Wickham should invent such a history of himself!" said Elizabeth. "Mr Bingley is a charming, amiable, sweet-tempered man and he cannot know what Darcy is. What is more, Darcy can please where he chooses—amongst those who are his equal in consequence, I wager he is a very different man from what he is to those less prosperous. He is probably sincere, rational, agreeable, even honourable—to those he deems worthy," she said sarcastically.

"Lizzy..." Jane chided her again. "Such strong expressions may be wholly undeserved. I urge you to temper your hostility towards Mr Darcy until such time as you may learn the truth behind the matter."

"Since I am unlikely to do so, I shall continue to think of him as I do," Elizabeth retorted. Then she gave her sister a grudging smile. "Very well, Jane. To please *you*, I shall attempt to reserve my judgement and not condemn Mr Darcy completely... yet." She paused, then frowned and added, "But Jane... do you think I ought not to have agreed to deliver the note to Mary King?"

"Why do you say that, Lizzy?"

"I just..." Elizabeth shrugged. "I feel slightly uneasy at my role of go-between. After all, I *am* breaking the rules of propriety in passing an illicit letter to Mary King without her uncle's knowledge or permission."

Jane was quiet for a moment, thinking. "There does seem to be good reason for such a letter, though," she said at last. "It would be cruel to leave Miss King in suspense, with no chance of a proper farewell."

"Yes. Those are my thoughts too," said Elizabeth, feeling reassured. "Very well, I shall attempt to find a convenient opportunity to pass the letter on to Mary King tomorrow evening."

CHAPTER TEN

Mr Bingley and his sister, Caroline, were staying with Mr and Mrs Hurst at their residence in Grosvenor Street during their time in London. The house was not quite as grand and elegant as the Darcys' townhouse, but it had a certain air of prestige—enough for Caroline Bingley to preen and preside with an air of great self-consequence as she stood by the front door greeting the guests as they arrived.

The dinner party was a fairly large affair, with many of the best families in town invited, though Elizabeth found the conversation at the dinner table dull and disappointing. Perhaps this was because she had been placed at the far end of the table, between several matrons who had little conversation beyond which debutante was coming out this season and which eligible bachelor was likely to be caught at last.

The rest of her party had fared better. Her aunt and uncle were sitting halfway up the table, next to Mary King and her uncle, and across from Mrs St John. Farther up still, at the other end, was her sister, Jane, who had been given the seat of honour next to Bingley. Together with them were Mr and Mrs Hurst, and Caroline Bingley, who had made sure to place Darcy by her side. Georgiana and her friend, Amy St John, completed the little group.

Elizabeth could not stop her eyes wandering down that side of the table several times during the meal and noticed Darcy smiling often at Amy, who was in remarkably good looks tonight. It seemed that Georgiana's transformation of her friend was well under way: instead of her usual dowdy faded attire, Amy was dressed in a lovely salmon-coloured silk gown which brought a rosy glow to her complexion; her hair was styled in a loose knot, with strands artfully pulled out and teased into curls to frame her face. In fact, she looked almost pretty and Elizabeth saw that not only Darcy but several of the other young men at the table were paying great attention to Amy. She was happy for the girl and she tried to ignore the uncomfortable prickle that stirred in her chest whenever she saw Darcy lean towards Amy.

By the time the ladies retired to the drawing room, Elizabeth was not in the best humour. She could not really understand why and she was angry with herself. Surely she was not resentful simply because a poor little country girl had managed to gain Darcy's attentions? No, it was not just that, she realised. There was a sense of hurt and disappointment that went deeper than envy. It was related to the incident with Wickham and the revelation of Darcy's true character. She had thought that he could be different—she had *wanted* him to be different... wanted to think she had misjudged him... heavens, wanted to *like* him! And then the encounter with Wickham in Hyde Park had shattered all her illusions. It seemed that Darcy was as arrogant and despicable as she had always thought him to be.

So why did she think of him still? Why did her eyes still drift across the room, looking for him? Why did she still wait for him to speak to her with something almost like anticipation? How could she feel anything but contempt and revulsion for such a man?

Her head was beginning to ache with the weight of her thoughts. Seeking a quiet moment away from the others, Elizabeth asked the footman for directions to the retiring room. There, she bathed her wrists and temples with some cool water brought by a maid and felt slightly better. As she was returning to the drawing room, she was distracted by a large doorway beside the main staircase. The door was slightly ajar and she caught a glimpse of a room filled with books. *This must be the Hurst's library!* she thought.

Elizabeth drifted towards the door and pushed it

open, slipping inside. She knew that she should not have entered uninvited, but she did not think anyone would miss her for a few moments. As a great lover of books, there was something powerfully attractive about the thought of an entire library unexplored. She would only have a brief look, she promised herself, and then she would return to the drawing room. But she had barely begun to peruse the titles on the shelves closest to her when she heard a step behind her.

"So you have abandoned the duty of conversation for the attractions of a book."

Elizabeth whirled around. Darcy had come into the library behind her. They stared at each other for a moment and Elizabeth was reminded of the time when she was staying in Netherfield Park and had inadvertently walked in on him in the billiards room. They had stood and stared at each other then, just as now, until she had dropped her eyes at last and left the room.

This time it was Darcy who was intruding upon her solitude, but he seemed in no hurry to quit the area. He advanced slowly into the room and Elizabeth found herself taking an unconscious step backwards. Annoyed at her own reaction, she stepped forwards again, so that she stood breast to breast with him as he came to a stop by the bookshelf. He was so tall that she had to tilt her head to look up at him and she found herself suddenly feeling strangely breathless.

"It is ironic to hear that rebuke from one who spurns conversation as much as you do," she said dryly.

Darcy inclined his head. "I certainly have not the talent, which some people possess, of conversing easily with strangers. I concede, I am not a loquacious character, but amongst close friends and family, I hope I am unbending enough in reserve as to give some pleasure in conversation."

"And amongst those who you feel are beneath your consequence, you do not hesitate to snub and humiliate in the most despicable manner," Elizabeth flung at him, all the pent-up feelings from earlier rushing to the surface.

His face changed, the smile leaving his eyes and a coldness coming over his features as he understood her implication. "You refer to the incident in Hyde Park yesterday."

"Anyone who witnessed that encounter could hardly refrain from remarking on your abominable behaviour towards Mr Wickham," said Elizabeth hotly.

Darcy's face hardened. "However reprehensible my behaviour may have seemed, there is good reason for it."

"What reason could there be to treat a man so humiliatingly in public?" demanded Elizabeth. "Is it not enough for you to have reduced Mr Wickham to his present circumstances?"

Darcy pressed his lips together. "I am not at

liberty to share the details. But rest assured that Wickham is not the amiable, honourable gentleman you think him to be. Indeed, he is the very opposite. I must ask you to take my word for it."

"I do not take your word at all," said Elizabeth scornfully. "You ask me to join you in denouncing a man's character when you will offer no proof of his wrong-doing. That is the height of conceit and arrogance!" She narrowed her eyes. "When I was at the Netherfield ball, Miss Bingley had the insolence to inform me that Mr Wickham is of low birth and nothing more than the son of your late father's steward—she seemed to think this reason enough to justify your behaviour. Is that your defence as well?" She shook her head angrily. "I hardly feel that being of low birth is crime enough to warrant such abuse. Indeed, I cannot help but feel for Mr Wickham—"

"You take an eager interest in that gentleman's concerns," snapped Darcy.

"Whoever knows what his misfortunes have been can help feeling an interest in him?"

"His misfortunes!" said Darcy contemptuously. "Oh yes, his misfortunes have been great indeed."

Elizabeth flushed at his mocking tone. "Yes! And they are of your doing! And you refuse to explain yourself. You have deprived a young man of the best years of his life and yet you treat the mention of his misfortunes with contempt and ridicule. But then— why should I be surprised? From the very beginning of my acquaintance with you, your manners impressed me with the fullest belief of your arrogance, your conceit, and your selfish disdain of the feelings of others! I—"

"Enough!" said Darcy through clenched teeth. "You have said quite enough, madam. Forgive me for having disturbed your peace."

Turning, he stalked towards the library door and slammed it shut behind him.

CHAPTER ELEVEN

The gentlemen had joined the ladies in the drawing room and there was a lively game of cards at play when Elizabeth returned. She blended into the back of the audience congregated around the card table and attempted to lose herself in the excitement of the game. But her thoughts kept returning to the recent scene in the library and she seethed with fury and indignation.

She stole a glance at Darcy, who was on the other side of the room. His face was set in its usual lines of reserved hauteur, but she fancied that she saw anger still smouldering in his dark eyes. *Good*, she thought, childishly pleased that he should be suffering as much vexation as she was.

After a while, Elizabeth's temper cooled

slightly and she attempted to distract herself by watching the card game. The table in front of her consisted of a set made up of Jane and Bingley, Caroline Bingley and Mary King. As her gaze drifted over the last, Elizabeth suddenly remembered her promise to Wickham. She had not yet had an opportunity to speak to Mary King in private and deliver the note to its rightful owner. Now she was beset by a feeling of unease.

Without Wickham's charming presence by her side, her discomfort about acting as go-between was growing. Was she doing the right thing? Though she was still furious at Darcy, his words in the library had sunk in. He had spoken with a heavy certainty which had touched her, in spite of herself. What if there was an element of truth in Darcy's accusations? Could she take responsibility for embroiling Mary King in scandal and danger?

But... what if she was letting Darcy's powerful presence influence her? She had promised Wickham that she would stand firm in her own opinions and now she was ashamed of how quickly she was wavering. What if Darcy was wrong and Wickham's intentions *were* noble and genuine? Perhaps Wickham's feelings for Mary King had led him to repent and redeem himself. She knew that if she spoke to Jane, her sister would urge strongly for allowances to be made and forgiveness attempted. Perhaps Wickham was sorry now for what he had done and anxious to re-establish his character. Then it would be wrong of her to deprive the lovers of their cherished goodbye.

She agonised over the decision as the others continued to cheer and talk and laugh over the card game. Finally, her eyes drifted once more across the room and met Darcy's dark gaze.

Their eyes locked for a long moment as Elizabeth's thoughts whirled in her head. Then she looked away again, her heart pounding uncomfortably in her chest. She was seized by a sudden urge to confide in Darcy. It was ludicrous, it was crazy—she was furious at him still—and yet at the same time, she felt as if he was the only person she could trust, the only person she could turn to in her present dilemma.

She made up her mind. Glancing back at Darcy, she gave him a long, speaking look. Then she turned and discreetly made her way across the drawing room to the adjoining music room. Georgiana and Amy were sitting in a corner, huddled together in their usual fashion, giggling over something in their hands. Elizabeth caught the glimpse of a piece of cream paper before Georgiana thrust it into her reticule and both girls looked up at her expectantly. Elizabeth favoured them with only the briefest of smiles before walking over to the pianoforte. A pile of sheet music lay atop one corner of the instrument and she occupied herself flipping through the pages until Darcy joined her a few moments later.

She was gratified that he had understood her silent plea for help so easily, though she was unsure what to do now that he was here. A long, awkward silence stretched between them, broken only by the giggling and whispering of Georgiana and Amy in the corner. The two girls had returned to their former preoccupation and seemed to be engrossed in passing a note back and forth between them. Elizabeth was glad that they did not seem to show any curiosity over why Darcy had joined her beside the pianoforte. Indeed, with the rest of the party engrossed by the card game, no one was paying them much attention and they were afforded a rare moment of privacy. It was too good an opportunity to lose.

Elizabeth took a deep breath and said in a small, embarrassed voice, "I have no right to ask this of you, Mr Darcy. However, I'm a selfish creature and I hope you will forgive me imposing upon your goodwill to ask for your advice and assistance."

"I am honoured to be asked," said Darcy quietly.

Quickly, Elizabeth informed him of Wickham's request and the note that she now held in her reticule.

"What does the note say?"

Elizabeth looked at him in horror. "I have not looked, sir! It is a private correspondence."

"It would be an easy way to determine Wickham's motives," said Darcy. "Forgive me, madam, but knowing what I do of Wickham's character, I have little patience in honouring his rights. In this case, I think the ends justify the means."

"Well…" Elizabeth did not want to argue with Darcy about Wickham's character again, but she did not feel comfortable with what he was suggesting.

"Give me the letter," Darcy commanded.

Elizabeth hesitated, then reached into her reticule and withdrew the note. It was on heavy cream paper, folded over twice, and perfumed with a light citrus fragrance. Darcy took it from her and rested it discreetly amongst the sheet music in front of them, so that no one else might observe what they were doing. Then he carefully unfolded it and they read it together:

My darling Mary,
*   It is with regret that I must write this letter and tell you that we must part. Your uncle feels me unworthy of you—and he may be*

justified in his belief. I am nothing but a simple officer with no fortune to my name. You deserve a life of greater wealth and comfort with another and I do not feel, in all conscience, that I could hold you to me for the sake of our love.

I shall always hold the memory of you in my heart and treasure the time we had together—but I ask you now to forget me and live your life in health and happiness. May God bless you.

Yours,
George Wickham

"So he did tell the truth..." Elizabeth murmured, her cheeks colouring slightly at the passionate words on the page. She felt guilty and embarrassed now, as if they had intruded on a private moment. "Wickham told me that it was a goodbye note to Mary King, to encourage her to forget him, and it is exactly as he said."

Darcy frowned but did not say anything.

"I must give this to Miss King. She deserves to have it," said Elizabeth, reaching for the note.

Darcy whisked it out of her reach. "No," he said, folding it and tucking it into his own inner coat pocket.

Elizabeth stared at him incredulously.

"Hand me the note, sir!" she hissed.

"No," said Darcy again. His face was bland. "I believe it can do more harm than good."

"But... but you saw what it said," protested Elizabeth. "Wickham told the truth! I should honour his request. Is it not bad enough that we should intrude on a couple's private correspondence—and now we are depriving them of their last goodbye as well?"

Darcy's tone was cool. "You may think as you wish, Miss Bennet, but you are not having the letter."

"Oooh!" Elizabeth had to resist the urge to stamp her foot in frustration. She glared at Darcy. All her anger and indignation came back. *Arrogant, overbearing swine!* "I should never have come to you!"

Turning, she stalked back to the drawing room, seething at Darcy's high-handedness. She was glad to see that the card game had finally broken up and that the guests were milling about. Good. Perhaps the evening would be coming to a close soon and they could leave. She did not think she had ever spent another evening as frustrating as this one and she was longing to return to Gracechurch Street and the peace and solitude of her bedroom. Then her eyes fell on Mary King, who was talking animatedly with Jane and Bingley. She felt her conscience prick her.

She had *promised* Wickham to deliver that letter. She could not go back on her word now, especially when he had been telling the truth in his request.

Elizabeth hesitated, then made up her mind. She walked across to Mary King and drew the girl aside. In a quiet undertone, she quickly recounted her meeting with Wickham in Hyde Park and his request that she pass on the message of goodbye.

"Where is the letter?" asked Mary King.

"Er... I no longer have it," said Elizabeth awkwardly. "But rest assured, Miss King, the message is exactly as I have recounted it."

The other girl narrowed her eyes. "How could you know the exact words? Did you read my private letter?"

Elizabeth flushed. "I... it fell out of my reticule and unfolded itself. Mr Wickham did not seal it. I could not help but glance at the message. It was only a short one."

"I want to see it for myself," said Mary King stubbornly.

"That is not possible," said Elizabeth. "I am sorry but I... er... I have lost the letter."

"Where?" demanded Mary King. "Where did you lose it? Perhaps I can go back and search for it—"

"Miss King, what does it matter? You know the contents now. Surely you—"

"No!" said Mary King wildly, her voice rising. "You don't understand. I *must* see the letter! The actual letter that Wickham wrote!"

Elizabeth glanced over her shoulder. People were starting to give them curious looks. She saw Darcy watching her sardonically.

"Shhh..." said Elizabeth, turning back to Mary King. "I beg you to calm yourself, Miss King."

"I must see the letter," said Mary King again, her voice ending on a slight sob.

Elizabeth could see tears filling the other girl's eyes and she felt racked by guilt. This was all her fault! If only she hadn't shown the letter to Darcy! He had no right confiscating it like that. Her mouth tightened.

"Listen," she said tersely. "Dry your tears now. People will start to wonder at your distress and there will be gossip. I... I will try to find a way to retrieve the letter for you."

Mary King sniffed. "Will... will you?"

Elizabeth hesitated, then nodded as a plan began forming in her mind. "I will do my best," she promised.

The other girl did not look reassured by these words and turned away, her shoulders slumping. A few minutes later, she left with her uncle, her head down, her expression wretched. Elizabeth felt guilt stab at her again. She was grateful when her aunt and uncle made their own excuses and they left the party a little later. The strain of trying to maintain polite conversation—and avoid Darcy's eyes—was becoming unbearable.

Once in the carriage on the way home, however, Elizabeth could not stop her thoughts returning to the look of devastation on Mary King's face. She felt miserable. She had failed the girl and she had failed Wickham.

I must do something to put this right, she thought grimly. *This is all my fault and now it is up to me to rectify it.*

CHAPTER TWELVE

Elizabeth took a deep breath and reached up to grasp the brass knocker on the front entrance of Darcy House. A moment later, the door swung open to reveal the impassive face of Manning, the Darcys' butler. He was standing stiff as a board and looked down his long nose at her with an expression of hauteur that almost rivalled Darcy's. His eyebrows rose slightly at seeing her standing on the doorstep, then she saw his eyes travel beyond her and his brows climbed even higher when he realised that she was unaccompanied and did not even have the company of a maid.

Elizabeth pinned her best smile on her face. "Good morning. I am here to call on Miss Darcy."

"I did not know that Miss Darcy was

expecting visitors this morning."

"Miss Darcy was kind enough to call upon me a few days ago, so I am returning the courtesy." Elizabeth let a hint of impatience slip into her tone and raised her chin, injecting some haughtiness into her own expression. "Are you planning to keep me waiting here on the front step all day?"

She crossed her fingers behind her back and hoped that Georgiana had not gone out. If the mistress was not at home, Elizabeth could do little more than leave a calling card and return to Gracechurch Street. However, it was still early in the day and she was banking on the fact that Georgiana probably kept town hours while she was in London so the chances of her having gone out already were slim.

Manning hesitated for a moment longer, then swung the door open and escorted her into the house. Elizabeth breathed a silent sigh of relief as she stepped in and was shown to the drawing room.

"I shall inform Miss Darcy that you are here," said Manning. He paused, then added delicately, "She may be detained slightly... *ahem...* by some... personal matters."

Elizabeth tried not to let her delight show. That meant that Georgiana was likely to be still in bed and would need some time to be roused, washed, and dressed. *Perfect.* Her assumption about the girl keeping town hours had been right. And this would give her exactly the opportunity she needed.

"That is no problem at all," she said to Manning, seating herself on one of the settees and picking up a book from the little side table. "I am at my leisure and have no other engagements this morning. Please advise Miss Darcy not to hurry on my account. I shall be pleased to await her here and... er... amuse myself with this book in the meantime. I began reading it at the soirée the other night and am keen to continue," she lied glibly. She paused, then asked as casually as she could, "Is Mr Darcy at home?"

"No, ma'am. The master has gone to his club and is not expected back until this evening," Manning said ponderously. He bowed, then retreated. Elizabeth waited until she heard his heavy footsteps fade away, then laid the book back down. She stood up and made her way stealthily to the drawing room doorway. Pressing her body against the wall, she leaned out slightly so that she could peek just beyond the edge of the wall. The hallway was empty.

Elizabeth drew back again and debated her next move. She knew the layout of the ground floor of Darcy House fairly well, having had a chance to wander through a few rooms during the soirée the other evening. She knew that the dining room lay at the end of the hall, then the library, then this drawing room, which adjoined the music room. But she had noticed another door that evening—a closed door on the opposite side of the hallway to the library. She had wondered at the time if it was Darcy's study. The place he would keep important documents and private letters. *Like the one Wickham wrote to Mary King.*

Elizabeth leaned out again and peered down the hallway once more. The path down to the dining room, with the library and the mysterious door on either side, was clear. She turned her head and looked the other way, back towards the front of the house. The hallway there expanded into a circular foyer, with high atrium ceilings and a curving staircase leading to the upper storeys. She could see no sign of Manning. No doubt there was a butler's post near the front door— perhaps off the foyer on the other side, hidden from view by the staircase. As long as Manning remained at his post, he would not be able to see this side of the house.

Elizabeth hesitated, biting her lip. The hallway was a long one and she would be completely exposed as she made her way down. If Manning should step away from his post for any reason, he would surely see her. On the other hand, it would not take her long to reach the other end and check the door opposite the library.

She had to try.

Taking a deep breath, Elizabeth stepped out into the hallway and began moving towards the other end, hugging the wall as she went. It was a silly gesture for she knew that the wall would afford her no cover should she be discovered, but it felt somehow better than walking straight down the exposed centre. She had to resist the urge to run flat out to the other end. Instead, she moved with slow, deliberate steps, her feet—clad in kid-leather slippers—moving soundlessly over the polished marble floor.

At last she was almost there—just a few steps away from that closed door—and then she heard a noise. Footsteps. From the foyer. Manning coming to check on her again? In a minute, he would round the side of the staircase and see her.

Elizabeth looked wildly around. There was no time to run back to the drawing room and he must not find her here, standing aimlessly in the hallway. She turned and ducked into the open doorway of the library. Quickly, she sidled up to a tall bookcase next to the door and held her breath.

What if Manning should go back into the drawing room? He would be expecting to find her there still and her absence would be sure to cause a stir. He would probably start to search the house for her. Elizabeth glanced about the library. If he found her here, she could placate him with a story about searching for a new book to read, though whether he would believe her was debatable. It would also appear highly inappropriate to trespass in a private library uninvited—however, it was the lesser of two evils. But although such a manoeuvre could have saved her, it would curtail her ability to search for Mary King's letter in Darcy's study and a second opportunity might have never presented itself.

Elizabeth gritted her teeth in frustration, her body tense as she listened to the footsteps coming closer and closer.

Closer and closer...

Elizabeth braced herself for Manning's appearance in the library doorway, but to her surprise, she saw a man walk past and continue down the hall. He was in liveried uniform and a powdered wig.

A footman, Elizabeth realised, breathing out in relief. He was carrying two silver candlestick holders and obviously heading for the dining room. She waited until his footsteps had faded away before peering out into the hallway again.

All clear. The footman had disappeared—perhaps to the kitchens and other servants' quarters, through a door on the other side of the dining room. And the foyer was still silent and empty. Manning was still at his post. Elizabeth hesitated. It was now or never.

She darted out and across the hall to the other door, putting her hand on the handle and turning it carefully. It was a heavy door and for a moment she thought it might be locked—then the resistance gave way and it opened. Flinging one last look over her shoulder, Elizabeth stepped inside and shut the door quietly behind her.

She was right—this was Darcy's study. It was decorated in a masculine style, with dark wood and leather accents. There was an enormous polished walnut desk dominating one end of the room, with a leather bergère armchair behind it and two upholstered chairs facing it. Several bookcases lined the walls and a large globe took pride of place in one corner.

Elizabeth crossed the room quickly. Her first object was Darcy's desk and she paused to scan its surface. There were various letters and other documents, a pile of books in one corner, a fat beeswax candle in a silver candlestick holder in the other, several sheets of foolscap paper in the centre of the desk flanked by a beautiful bronze-and-ormolu pen and ink set bearing glass inkwells, an ornate seal, a silver pen knife, and a large goose feather quill pen.

Elizabeth hesitated. Until this moment, she

had not thought much about what she would actually be *doing*. She had acted purely on impulse, driven by the excitement of an idea which had occurred to her the previous night. All her energies had centred on getting into Darcy's study. But now that she was here, she felt the sudden weight of guilt and shame.

She knew that she was trespassing terribly—she should not have been in here at all and to actually start rifling through Darcy's private things seemed utterly reprehensible. Furthermore, should she be caught by Manning or another servant, she would never live down the humiliation and scandal. She might even be judged to be behaving in a criminal manner and subject to arrest and interrogation!

The thought made her recoil from the desk and, for one moment, Elizabeth contemplated retreating to the drawing room. If she left now, no one would be any wiser of her uninvited tour of the house and the whole sorry escapade could be forgotten.

But no. Elizabeth steeled her spine. She was here now and she did not want to waste the opportunity. In any case, she reminded herself, she was not stealing something that belonged to another. No indeed, she was simply retrieving what belonged to her. Wickham had given her the note for safekeeping and it was hers by right, until she delivered it to Mary King. Darcy had had no right to take it from her last night. His refusal to return it gave her every right to come and seek the item herself.

Elizabeth took a deep breath, then began searching through the desk, lifting some of the books to peek underneath, shuffling through the papers, looking in vain for any sign of the note with Wickham's handwriting. There was nothing.

Heaving a sigh of frustration, she turned to the bookcases next to the table, which held a variety of volumes on different topics. Art, travel, politics, history... she scanned the shelves, running her fingers across the spines of the books. Nothing. Of course, the letter could have been tucked away between the pages of a particular volume, but short of pulling each one out and rifling through the pages, there was no way she could know. In any case, the fine layer of dust on the tops of the books suggested that most had not been moved for some time.

Elizabeth turned back to the desk in frustration, then dropped into a crouch as she heard a sudden noise outside. Voices. Male voices, faint and muffled. It sounded like Manning was talking to someone in the foyer. Perhaps giving further instructions to the footmen. Elizabeth relaxed slightly, but was reminded of the urgency of her situation. She did not have much time. Georgiana would be coming down soon. Elizabeth glanced at the clock on the study wall and thought of her own simple morning routine. But a girl like Georgiana, attended by maids and expected to maintain a certain standard of appearance, was likely to have a much more complicated *toilette* and require much more time to get ready. She certainly hoped so.

Elizabeth rose slowly from her crouched position behind the desk, then froze halfway, her eyes riveted on the side of the desk. There was a shallow drawer beneath the centre section that she had not noticed earlier. It had a lock but there was a key in the keyhole.

She reached forwards, turned the key, and pulled out the drawer. It was filled with various letters and documents... then she saw it. Tucked into the corner. She recognised the thick cream paper with the scalloped edges. Quickly, she pulled it out of the drawer and unfolded it.

Yes, it was Wickham's note. Elizabeth folded it again and then realised that she had left her reticule in the drawing room. Her gown had no pockets. Irritated with herself, she folded the note once more until it was a small square which she tucked into the palm of one hand. Then she shut the drawer, locked it, and rose to her feet.

Swiftly, she made her way back across the room to the door of the study. She just had to get back to the drawing room, have as short a visit as possible with Georgiana, and then return to Gracechurch Street. Her aunt and Jane would be wondering where she was by now. They had still been abed when she left the house this morning and although she had left them a note saying that she was going to Lackington Allen & Co, the renowned booksellers at Finsbury Square, she knew that they would grow worried at a long absence.

She reached out for the door handle but, to her horror, saw that it was turning already. Someone was coming in from the other side!

The study door swung open and Elizabeth found herself face to face with Darcy.

CHAPTER THIRTEEN

"Miss Bennet."

She saw surprise flare in Darcy's eyes. He frowned. "May I ask—what are you doing in my study?"

"I... that is..." Elizabeth flushed. She groped wildly for a suitable excuse, a fitting lie, then she took a look at Darcy's face and decided that the truth was the best solution. She raised her chin and met his eyes evenly. "I came to retrieve something which was taken from me."

Darcy's eyes hardened. "I had not thought you the type to trespass in private areas of people's houses and rifle through their personal documents."

"Since you took something forcibly from me without my approval or permission, I consider us even," snapped Elizabeth. "I would have no need to be here, engaging in such furtive activities, if you had behaved in a more gentlemanlike manner."

Darcy stiffened, then he shut the door behind him and moved across to his desk.

"I concede that perhaps my action last night in appropriating the letter was not warranted. Perhaps such behaviour was beneath me. However, it was done for the best. On this subject, I have nothing more to say and no other apology to offer."

Elizabeth bristled at his high-handed manner. "That is hardly good enough, sir!"

Darcy sighed. "I have my reasons for confiscating the letter. I believe that it presents a danger to Mary King and that you would do harm should you deliver it into her hands."

"But you saw the letter!" said Elizabeth. "It was merely a message of goodbye! What harm could there be in that?"

"I do not trust Wickham. You do not know him as I do."

"So you keep saying!" Elizabeth exhaled in frustration. "And whose fault is that, pray? I would know him as well as you if you would but explain your reasons to me. How can you expect me to believe your condemnation of Wickham's character when you will not offer any proof of your reasoning?"

Darcy hesitated, then he shook his head. "I

must ask you to trust me, Miss Bennet. In any case, why should you still need the letter? I saw you speaking to Mary King last night. I assume that you conveyed Wickham's message to her."

"That is the very point," said Elizabeth impatiently. "Mary King insists on seeing the letter. Indeed, she was frantic. She will not accept my verbal account of Wickham's message. She insisted on seeing the letter for herself and became most distressed when I could not accommodate her." Elizabeth swallowed and looked down. "I was racked by guilt. I felt that it was my fault that Mary King had lost her final farewell from the man she loves. So I determined to retrieve the letter and deliver it to her, as I originally intended."

Elizabeth looked back up and was surprised to see that Darcy did not seem to be listening to her. Instead, he appeared to be deep in thought, his expression distant.

"You say that Mary King asked to see the physical letter?" he said at last.

Elizabeth nodded.

Darcy frowned. "Why? Why should that be so important to her?"

Elizabeth shrugged. "It is hardly surprising. It would be a romantic memento of Wickham's feelings for her, I imagine. Besides, there is often a desire to see a message with one's own eyes to believe its authenticity."

Darcy gave an impatient shake of his head. "No, I believe it may be more than that."

"What do you mean?"

He held out his hand. "May I ask to see the letter again, Miss Bennet?" He saw her hesitate and added impatiently, "I will not annex it again. I give you my word of honour that I shall return it to you—but I must examine it again."

Elizabeth stretched her hand out slowly and opened her palm to show him the folded piece of paper tucked there. Darcy took it from her, their fingers brushing slightly, and Elizabeth felt a jolt of awareness at the contact. Darcy appeared unmoved, however. He was busy unfolding the letter. Pushing her own heightened awareness of him away, Elizabeth stepped closer and watched as Darcy spread the letter open in front of them.

"I do not see anything different from last night," she remarked, her eyes scanning the words on the page. She sniffed appreciatively. "Indeed, the lemon fragrance that Wickham applied is most potent still. It is a lovely scent—I wonder where he might have obtained such a fragrance?"

"The lemon scent..." Darcy mused. He turned suddenly and reached for the candle on his desk. He lit it.

"What... What are you doing?" asked

Elizabeth in alarm. She saw him bring the candle closer to the letter. "You are not burning it!"

"Rest easy, Miss Bennet. I gave you my word that I would return the letter to you and I shall. I will not damage it. But I believe that it contains more than we are seeing."

"I beg your pardon? I do not take your meaning."

"These words,..." Darcy gestured to the letter with his other hand. "I do not think this is the only message that Wickham is sending to Mary King."

Elizabeth frowned. "But... what else could there be?"

"There is another message. Hidden. Written between these lines, I believe—in invisible ink."

"Invisible ink?" laughed Elizabeth. "No, that is too absurd."

"We shall see in a moment if I am right," said Darcy.

Carefully, he lifted the note and held it directly above the candle flame—close enough to the heat but not close enough to singe the paper. Elizabeth gasped as dark brown writing began to appear in the blank spaces between the previously written lines.

"But... I do not understand... How do the words appear like that?"

"They were written in lemon juice,"

explained Darcy. "The scent gave it away. It is a well-known method of hiding a message. When mixed with water and applied carefully to paper, it dries in such a way as to be invisible to the naked eye. But once subjected to heat, the properties of the juice changes so that it is rendered brown and obvious."

Elizabeth leaned forwards to read the new message revealed on the paper and drew a sharp intake of breath.

My darling Mary,

I long each day for the time when we may be together as man and wife. I know your uncle's objections can hold no obstacles to our love. I am yours and I await your bidding—only give me a sign and we shall be together. Indeed, I fear that if we do not make the move soon, there will be those who will scheme to come between us. If you value our love, then do not delay. You know the place in the park. Send me word to meet you there and I shall come to carry you away.

Yours,
George Wickham

"So... Wickham is up to his old tricks again," said Darcy grimly as he read the message. "It is clear that he is attempting to coerce Miss King into an elopement."

Elizabeth shook her head, her eyes still on the letter, not wanting to believe the truth about Wickham. "No... there must be some mistake. Surely Wickham could not be so depraved..." She looked desperately at Darcy. "Perhaps... perhaps we have read too much into this message. After all, there is no mention of Gretna Green. Perhaps these are merely words of passionate frustration..." She trailed off weakly.

Darcy's lips tightened. "I am sorry to destroy your illusions of Mr Wickham, Miss Bennet, but he is more than capable of such evil."

He turned from her suddenly and paced to the other side of the room, then turned and came back. Elizabeth watched him in wonder. He appeared to be wrestling with a decision. At last, Darcy paused again in front her.

"I know what Wickham is capable of because... this is not the first time he has attempted such a seduction."

Elizabeth stared at him. "How can you know that?"

Darcy's eyes were bleak. "Because the last time he attempted to do the same, it was with my sister, Georgiana."

CHAPTER FOURTEEN

Elizabeth gasped and took an involuntary step backwards. "No..."

"Yes," said Darcy. He hesitated, then added, "I must now mention a circumstance which I would wish to forget myself, and which no obligation less than the present emergency should induce me to unfold to anyone."

He walked away from her again to the study windows and stood gazing out, his face harsh and grim. He seemed to be lost in thought for a moment, then at last he began to speak. Elizabeth's eyes widened with shock and horror as she listened to his account and compared it to the one she had heard. That Wickham was the son of the late Mr Darcy's steward and had been promised a valuable family living, with the church as his profession, was certainly true. But there the similarity between the two stories ended. It transpired that Wickham had in fact resolved against taking orders and had asked for—and been given—a sum of £3,000 in lieu, as compensation. This, in addition to the £1,000 which was his legacy, should have been sufficient to support him in any career he chose. However, a life of idleness and dissipation had led to him frittering away his inheritance and duly returning to Darcy for more funds. When this application was refused, Wickham had become resentful and vindictive. He turned his thoughts to revenge—which came in the form of compromising Darcy's younger sister.

"Compromise Miss Darcy!" cried Elizabeth, horrified.

Darcy nodded grimly. "He arranged to meet her whilst she was staying in Ramsgate last summer and persuaded her to believe herself in love with him and to consent to an elopement. She was then but fifteen and the ensuing scandal would no doubt have ruined her for life. Fortunately, I arrived in time to prevent the worst and to protect her reputation from public exposure. Wickham abandoned her immediately, as his real object was unquestionably her fortune of £30,000—as well as the wish to revenge himself on me." His mouth twisted. "I hope this will acquit me henceforth of cruelty towards Mr Wickham. I can only humbly ask that you respect the discretion required to keep my sister's reputation safe."

"I... I... Of course," stammered Elizabeth.

She was beset by a tumult of emotions—a mixture of shock, horror, disbelief, and shame. She realised now how much she had wronged Darcy. She thought back to her encounters with Wickham and she was struck now by the impropriety of much of his conduct, particularly the way he had put himself forward with the story of his abuse at the hands of Mr Darcy. He had no reserves, no scruple in sinking Mr Darcy's character, though he had assured her that respect for the father would always prevent his exposing the son.

Suddenly she saw Wickham with wholly new eyes. How differently everything appeared now! *How unjustly have I acted*, she thought. *I who have prided myself on my discernment! I who have valued myself on my abilities!* She remembered Jane's gentle remonstrance in the park and her sister's generous allowances for misinterpretations of intentions and character. How right Jane had been!

Had I been in love, I could not have been more wretchedly blind, thought Elizabeth miserably. *But vanity, not love has been my folly. Flattered by Wickham's attentions and offended by Darcy's neglect, I have laid myself open to prejudice in such a manner as I have always despised in others.*

"Thank you for taking me into your confidence," she said to Darcy at last. "I am very sensible of the honour and, of course, I give you my word that I will maintain the utmost discretion regarding Miss Darcy's past involvement with Wickham." She hesitated, then indicated the letter once more. "What should I do about this? I certainly cannot give it to Miss King now. Indeed, I am relieved I never attempted it. I should not like to have been responsible for a scandal of this magnitude and the ruin of her good name." She looked at him hopefully. "Perhaps—as Mary King has not received this letter—she may as yet be safe. We could simply leave matters as they are."

"I wish I could agree, Miss Bennet," said Darcy. "But I do not trust Wickham and I feel that he would find another method to reach Miss King. I feel that we are obliged to warn Mary King's uncle of his intentions."

"Will he believe us?"

"I understand that Horace King is already ill disposed towards Wickham. Indeed, that is the reason he removed Miss King from Meryton so abruptly and brought her to London. Thus, he may need very little convincing." Darcy paused, then said, "It may be best if I paid him a private visit. I shall endeavour to pass on my suspicions of Wickham's intentions without exposing my own sister's involvement this affair. I am hopeful that he will not ask for proof of Wickham's guilt as assiduously as you have done." He gave Elizabeth a wry smile.

She flushed. "And if you should need to show the letter, how will you explain your possession of it?"

Darcy hesitated.

"You may tell Horace King that *I* gave it to you," said Elizabeth. "I shall take responsibility for it. It is the least I can do. You may tell him that Wickham asked me to play messenger, but I was uneasy with the role and so I came to you for assistance."

She did not add that Horace King would no doubt wonder why she should go to Darcy for assistance—it suggested an intimacy of friendship that did not actually exist. However, if Darcy thought the same, he did not comment.

He shook his head. "As I said, I shall endeavour to avoid introducing this letter if possible, and thus any mention of your involvement. I appreciate your willingness to take responsibility in this matter, but the fault is not yours and I should not like you to suffer any consequences in connection with this." He handed her the letter. "Keep this. It is yours. And do not worry—I shall find a means to convince Horace King of Wickham's infamy, though I do not think I shall have to try too hard." He gave a grim smile, then turned towards the study door. "And now, I must go. It is fortunate that my business was concluded more swiftly than I anticipated. I had not expected to be home until this evening but now I am free to call on Horace King."

Elizabeth followed him to the door. She was conscious of a great sense of relief in having Darcy's help in the matter, and also felt immense gratitude that he had not let her recent churlish behaviour prevent him from helping her. Darcy was far more noble and generous than she!

He paused by the door and looked at her. "I shall attempt to let you know how things progress. Perhaps I can send word to Gracechurch Street..." He hesitated, no doubt remembering that a gentleman may not write to a lady without causing gossip. "Perhaps it may be best if I send the message anonymously."

"Thank you," said Elizabeth, grateful for his thoughtful consideration. She thought of how unjustly she had condemned and upbraided him and felt a new wave of shame at her own conduct. She had been utterly mistaken in his character and suddenly she longed to apologise, to ask for his forgiveness.

Some of her turmoil must have shown in her eyes, for Darcy gave her a gentle smile—though he misunderstood the cause of her distress. "Do not look so, Miss Bennet. All is not lost. I have confidence that I will speak to Horace King and disaster may be averted."

He reached out and caught hold of her hand, squeezing it reassuringly. Elizabeth caught her breath, her heart pounding. She was suddenly aware of how close they were standing. They were facing each other, beside the door, and she could almost feel the heat from his body. Darcy smiled at her, his eyes soft, and Elizabeth felt herself sway towards him.

Then a knock sounded sharply next to them, making her jump. Darcy took a step back and Elizabeth felt a strange sense of disappointment. The next moment, the door opened to reveal Manning standing there. His long face registered shock and disapproval as his eyes fell on Elizabeth.

"Miss Bennet! I did not think you would be in Mr Darcy's private study." He pursed his lips. "I understood you to be awaiting Miss Darcy in the drawing room."

Elizabeth groped desperately for an

explanation. "Well, I... um..."

"I invited Miss Bennet to accompany me to my study, Manning," Darcy spoke up. "I wished to know her opinion on a book and brought her here to show it to her."

"Perhaps next time, the book could be taken to Miss Bennet in the drawing room, sir," said Manning primly.

"You're absolutely right, Manning," said Darcy with an amused look. "I shall certainly remember your suggestion for the next time. But now I must go out again. Please can you fetch my hat and coat—and inform Miss Darcy that Miss Bennet will join her in the drawing room shortly."

"Very good, sir." Manning bowed again, then shooting another suspicious look at Elizabeth, he turned and stalked back down the hallway.

As they heard his footsteps fading away, Darcy chuckled under his breath and said to Elizabeth, "Do not mind him. Manning is a great stickler for propriety, but he is a good man."

He began to turn away but Elizabeth put a hand on his arm, stopping him.

"Darcy..." She blushed slightly and removed her hand from his arm. "I... Thank you. Thank you for trusting me and confiding in me about your sister... in... in spite of the way I behaved... I mean, the things I said about you... and Wickham... I am most heartily ashamed of myself," she stammered, unable to meet his eyes.

Darcy regarded her for a moment, then smiled gently. "Do not distress yourself, Miss Bennet. It is all forgotten."

With a bow, he left the room and was gone. Elizabeth returned to the drawing room and drifted to the windows. She was just in time to see Darcy mounting his horse and spur it into a fast trot. Her heart full of an emotion she could not name, she watched him until he had disappeared around the corner and out of sight.

CHAPTER FIFTEEN

"Miss Bennet. I beg your pardon for keeping you waiting," Georgiana said, curtsying in the drawing room doorway. She was dressed in a pretty morning gown of lemon yellow, trimmed with white Belgian lace, and her hair was arranged in a becoming fashion, with curls trailing down over one shoulder. Her cheeks were flushed and, though her appearance was immaculate, she appeared slightly flustered. Elizabeth imagined that she must have risen and dressed in the utmost hurry and she felt a pang of guilt.

"No, it is I who should ask for forgiveness, Miss Darcy," she said quickly. "I should not have called upon you so early. I am afraid I am used to country routines and forgot that those in town keep later hours."

"Oh no, not at all. I should have been awakening anyway." Georgiana gave her a rueful smile as she came into the room and joined Elizabeth on the sofa. "I confess, 'tis all these late-night parties that I am not used to."

"Did you continue for much longer after we had left last night?" asked Elizabeth.

"Oh no, not for very much longer," said Georgiana. "Indeed, we were back at Darcy House a little after midnight. But I... well... I could not sleep last night. I was feeling quite... exhilarated."

Elizabeth smiled. She had not thought that anyone else could have experienced as exciting an evening as herself last night, nor struggled so much to sleep afterwards, with a head full of turbulent thoughts. But she had forgotten what it was like to be sixteen and having your first taste of society—to finally be able to converse with others and be treated as an adult, to enjoy the dinners and card games and little flirtations... She thought of her own younger sisters, Kitty and Lydia, and their anticipation of balls and dances, their delight at the attention of the officers, their excitement at receiving compliments and admiration...

And there had been several eligible young men at the party last night, such as Lord Denning and his cousin, Henry Ashley. Elizabeth had noticed them flirting outrageously with Amy and Georgiana and doing their best to compete for the young ladies' attentions. Her smile widened. She was not surprised that such an evening would leave Darcy's sister feeling too euphoric to sleep.

"It is extremely gratifying to capture a gentleman's attention, is it not?" she said, giving Georgiana a mischievous smile. "One feels almost giddy with so much influence."

"Yes!" cried Georgiana, her eyes sparkling. "I am so glad you can understand my feelings, Miss Bennet! To inspire so much love and admiration... it is beyond my wildest dreams! I had thought such sentiments only existed in romantic novels, but then to discover that they could be real... and that I could excite them! Oh, it was the most exhilarating discovery. I could hardly sleep a wink last night!"

"Er..." Elizabeth was slightly taken aback by the girl's vehemence. She had not realised that the flirtations had become so serious. She hoped that the girl's affections were fixed more on Lord Denning than Henry Ashley. The latter, though amiable and wealthy in his own right, was only a second son and would not be able to lay claim to the bulk of his father's vast estate. She did not think that Darcy would agree to such a match for his sister.

"Um... does your brother know of your feelings?" she asked.

"No." A shadow crossed Georgiana's face. "And I shall not tell him, for he would not understand."

Elizabeth shifted uncomfortably. She felt thrust suddenly into the role of an Older Person and whilst she did not feel it in her place to interfere with the Darcys' family affairs, she felt obliged to defend Darcy in his absence. "You know, your brother wishes nothing but the best for you," she said gently.

"Yes, I know," Georgiana looked away. "But he does not always know what *is* best for me."

"Miss Darcy—"

"Oh, I know Fitzwilliam is good to me. Indeed, in many ways, he is an ideal older brother but…" She shook her head, looking down at her hands. "Sometimes I think he takes his role as my guardian too seriously. He gives me no credit for knowing my own mind."

"Perhaps if you talked to him—"

"No," said Georgiana sadly. "He would not understand."

Elizabeth started to say more but was interrupted by Manning appearing in the drawing room doorway.

"Miss St John is here to see you, Miss Georgiana." He stepped back to let the young lady enter the room.

"Amy!" cried Georgiana in delight, jumping up and hurrying over to grasp the other girl's hands.

"Georgie, I must tell you… I have been thinking about the message and I think—"

Georgiana gave a jerk and Amy broke off. Her gaze slid past Georgiana's shoulder and fell on Elizabeth.

"Oh! I did not realise that you were here, Miss Bennet." She coloured.

Elizabeth rose. The two girls' affection for each other was obvious and she felt a little as if she was intruding. "I am not staying long. Indeed, I believe I should leave now. My aunt and sister will be wondering where I am. It has been a pleasure seeing you again, Miss Darcy—"

"Oh, please… do not leave on my account," cried Amy.

"Yes, please do stay for some refreshment at least," urged Georgiana.

Elizabeth hesitated, then agreed. Georgiana rang the bell for tea, then the three young ladies sat down. Conversation soon flowed easily as they shared their impressions of the capital and discussed the latest fashions. Though they were much younger, Elizabeth found Georgiana and Amy to be delightful company and their youthful enthusiasm infectious.

"Only fancy! I heard that Lady Caroline Lamb has cut off all her hair!" Georgiana said, her eyes wide. "It is nothing more than a shorn cap of curls on her head now. I have not seen her, but I have heard that it is *most* becoming. Indeed, I was wondering if I should consider such a hairstyle myself…" She fingered her blonde curls.

"You would not!" Amy stared at her friend in scandalised horror.

Georgiana giggled. "I would! Though I do not think Fitzwilliam would let me. He is so very proper sometimes. What say you, Miss Bennet? Would you ever consider such a controversial style?" She turned to Elizabeth.

"The controversy would not sway me," said

Elizabeth with a smile. "But I do not think that I should like to have my hair short. 'Tis most soothing to brush the locks out before bed each night."

"Yes," Georgiana agreed. "And one might risk looking *unfeminine* with such short hair, do you not think? My brother always says that a woman's hair is one of her chief sources of beauty."

"Oh, then I am excessively glad that I have kept all of mine," said Amy fervently. "And I am most grateful, Georgiana, for your help in styling it so much more becomingly!"

Elizabeth looked at the young country girl and saw that the transformation which she had witnessed the night before had continued. Amy was wearing a demure morning dress of sprigged muslin, but the simple cut enhanced her figure and the blue satin ribbon around the bodice brought out the colour of Amy's pale blue eyes. Her hair was dressed in a loose knot again, with a matching blue satin ribbon woven amongst the fine strands. She looked fresh-faced and pretty, and Elizabeth marvelled at the change in her.

"If I might be allowed to say so, Miss St John, you are in remarkably good looks," she said to Amy with a warm smile.

The other girl blushed. "Oh… thank you! I have Georgiana to thank for everything." She gestured to her gown. "This is one of the generous gifts that has been bestowed on me."

"Wait until you see the riding habit I am having

altered for you," said Georgiana excitedly. "Then you shall inflame all the gentlemen when you go riding in Hyde Park!"

"Do you like to ride, Miss St John?" said Elizabeth. "I confess, I much prefer to walk."

"Oh, I enjoy riding prodigiously!" said Amy, beaming. "And now I can indulge my passion, thanks to the kindness of Mr Darcy."

Elizabeth looked puzzled and Amy hurried to explain. "Mr Darcy has arranged for me to have the use of a pony from the liveried stables whilst I am in town. Is that not wonderfully generous of him?" She smiled at Georgiana. "He overheard me last night when I was speaking of my love of riding and how I missed the activity since coming to London. As Mrs St John does not keep a horse in town, I did not think I would have the opportunity. But now I shall be able to go for early morning rides in the park, thanks to your brother's arrangements."

"That is very charitable of him," said Elizabeth, surprised at Darcy's generous action towards the other girl.

"Yes, Fitzwilliam often does such things," said Georgiana with a smile. "With those he holds in high regard, he is most benevolent and kind."

"I am honoured to be admitted to that intimate group," said Amy, blushing.

Elizabeth was suddenly aware of that uncomfortable feeling in her breast again. She would normally celebrate and not envy others their good fortune and happiness, so why did she feel such a wave of resent towards Amy? Ashamed of her own feelings, she hurriedly set down her teacup.

"This has been a most delightful interlude, but I fear I really must take my leave now." Elizabeth stood up and picked up her reticule. "Thank you for your hospitality, and I hope to see you again soon." She curtsied. "Miss Darcy... Miss St John."

The girls returned the curtsy, then Elizabeth followed Manning quietly to the front door and was shown out of the house.

CHAPTER SIXTEEN

Horace King's residence was a respectable-looking house in Mayfair. Darcy presented himself at the front door and was relieved to hear that the master was at home. He was shown into the study where he was met by a middle-aged man with bushy eyebrows and a lugubrious expression.

"Mr Darcy." Horace King held his hand. "This is an honour. What can I do for you?"

"I fear the reason for my visit is not a pleasant one," said Darcy. Quickly, he apprised the older man of the situation. King's bushy eyebrows drew together as he listened and his face grew red with indignation.

"The scoundrel!" he said, slamming a fist on his desk. "I had thought there was something fishy about Wickham. Couldn't put my finger on it, but that was why I removed Mary from Meryton society and had her brought to London. Nonetheless, I had not thought him as bold as this!"

"May I ask, sir—where is your niece?"

King frowned. "In her room, I imagine. She has taken to having breakfast in bed and keeping town hours. She does not normally make an appearance until mid-afternoon."

"Would you oblige me by confirming that, sir?" asked Darcy.

Horace King looked at him with sudden suspicion. "You don't think...?"

Darcy gave a shrug. "One merely wishes to ascertain that she is safe."

"Aye, of course," said King. He flung the study door open and called for the butler to send a maid up to his niece's quarters. A few moments later, the maid returned and one look at her face told Darcy that his suspicions had been right.

"If you please, sir..." The maid fingered her apron nervously. "Miss King is not in her chambers."

Horace King stared at her. "What do you mean not in her chambers?" He turned and roared for the butler again and soon every servant was scurrying about the house, looking for his Mary King. Darcy was not surprised when all the reports returned in the negative.

All save one—one of the chambermaids admitted seeing Mary King leave early that morning, with her lady's maid accompanying her.

"Well, at least she has her maid with her," said Horace King heavily. "That may help to alleviate the gossips a bit."

Darcy turned to the maid. "Do you know where they were heading?"

"I think they were headin' for some park, sir," said the girl. "I heard Sandra—that's Miss King's maid—grumblin' 'bout how she hates walkin' along the water on account of the bird droppin's that's there and it be stainin' the bottom of Miss King's gowns an' then 'tis a nightmare to wash it out—"

"She must be talking about the Serpentine in Hyde Park," said Darcy suddenly. "That is the only body of water nearby with a large population of waterfowl." He turned back to Horace King. "Is your niece in the habit of taking early morning walks in Hyde Park?"

"Well, I never thought so..." spluttered the man. "As far as I knew, she always kept to her rooms in the morning and only appeared after lunch. Of course, I am often away myself in the mornings so I cannot be certain of her exact movements." He paused and added, "I have taken her to Hyde Park on occasion—but it has always been in the afternoon, during the fashionable hour."

"Then it is highly suspicious that she should want to go now," said Darcy "I hate to be the bearer of bad tidings, but I fear that your niece may be attempting an assignation with Mr Wickham."

Horace King looked stunned. "An assignation?"

"Yes," said Darcy. "I have reason to believe that Wickham may attempt to coerce her into an elopement."

For a moment, he wondered if Horace King would demand proof of such an accusation, but to his relief, the man seemed too shocked to think of anything else.

"An elopement! No... No... That would be... Mary would be completely ruined!" he said, his face ashen. "We must stop them!"

"We must leave at once," said Darcy. "If we go to Hyde Park now, we may yet be in time."

For a moment, he thought Horace King was about to suffer an apoplexy—so purple was the man's face—but then, to his relief, the older man seemed to get a grip on himself.

"Yes, yes..." he muttered, snatching up his hat and coat. "We must catch them before it is too late."

They arrived at Hyde Park in record time, entering through the Apsley gates at Hyde Park Corner and making for the south bank of the

Serpentine. There was, in fact, nothing snake-like about the ornamental lake—which was created at the behest of Queen Caroline, the wife of George II—it had but one curve. However, it did have the distinction of being the first artificial lake to follow a more natural shape, at a time when most man-made lakes were constructed to be long and straight. It was formed by damming the Westbourne River and provided opportunities for many recreational activities, such as swimming, boating, and promenading along its banks.

It was this last activity that Darcy focused on now. There was a path along the northern bank known as the Ladies Mile—a more popular route for the ladies to promenade along—and he had a hunch that Mary King could be found there. He kicked his horse into a canter now as he skirted the side of the lake, with King following suit.

Darcy scanned the grassy walks and footpaths alongside the water as he rode past, hoping for a sign of the young lady. At this time of the day, the park was relatively empty—being too early yet for the fashionable set to come and parade themselves—but also too late for the grooms who brought their horses to exercise in the park before breakfast. It should have been easy to spot a lone young lady with her maid in tow.

"There!" said Darcy, pointing suddenly.

Horace King rode alongside, squinting into the distance. They saw two figures by the edge of the water: Mary King and her maid. The servant girl was standing nervously, whilst her mistress paced up and down the same spot. She heard the sound of hooves approaching and looked up, her expression hopeful. Then she recognised her uncle and her eyes filled with dismay.

"Mary! What are you doing here?" Horace King demanded.

Mary King picked up her skirts, a look of panic coming over her face. For a moment, Darcy thought she would turn and flee. Then her shoulders slumped and she stood with her head hanging miserably as they dismounted next to her.

Mary King's bottom lip wobbled. "I... I thought he would come for me..."

"You little fool!" said her uncle angrily. "You would have thrown your future away and for what? For a cad who is interested in nothing but your fortune."

"That is not true!" Mary King cried. "He loves me! I know he loves me! If you had not been so cruel as to prevent me from seeing him, we would not have needed to resort to such measures."

"Enough of that, my girl," Horace King

thundered. "You will come home with me at once and we will not speak of this incident again!" He glanced at the maid, who had been standing to the side, trying to appear as unobtrusive as possible. "Thank goodness you had the sense to bring your maid with you. At least you were never unchaperoned. Let us hope that this incident can be hushed up and no one will be wiser."

He glanced at Darcy, who had walked a discreet distance away, and went over to him.

"Sir, I am indebted to you for bringing this situation to my attention. Were it not for your timely warning and quick action, we may not have got here in time..." King grimaced.

Darcy scanned the landscape around them. "No sign of Wickham. Perhaps he saw us from a distance and decided on a quick retreat."

King jutted his chin out. "If that bounder dares to come near my niece again, he'll be sorry," he growled.

The two men shook hands, then Darcy mounted his horse and headed out of the park. He thought suddenly of Elizabeth and how she must be anxious to hear the outcome of his mission. He would write to her as soon as he returned home, he decided.

As he entered Darcy House, he was met by Manning and learned that he had just missed Miss Bennet. She had left barely a quarter of an hour ago, the butler reported, and his sister had departed not long after.

Damn, thought Darcy in frustration. Well, there was nothing for it but to send Elizabeth a message. He headed for his study and sat down at his writing desk to pen her a brief note. However, he found himself hesitating with the quill poised over the paper. Why send an anonymous note? Would it not be better for him to simply call at Gracechurch Street and give her the news in person?

He imagined how Elizabeth's face would look when he told her of Mary King's safe retrieval from Wickham's clutches and smiled to himself, anticipating the pleasure that he would give her. He glanced at the clock on the wall, then rose decisively. He would go now and hope that the Gardiners had no other engagements.

Darcy strode into the foyer, calling to Manning to have his horse brought round. He was aware that his pulse had increased at the thought of seeing Elizabeth again. He was glad now that he had confided in her regarding Georgiana's narrow escape and that they no longer had any secrets between them. He remembered that intimate moment in his study, before Manning had interrupted them, and his heart beat even faster. All the arguments he had put forth to Bingley—the inappropriateness of the family, the lack of fortune, the inferior social connections—were still there in his head, but they were like dim echoes, fading slowly away. He was not even listening to them anymore.

All he knew was that he was going to see the one woman who challenged him, exasperated him... and utterly entranced him.

CHAPTER SEVENTEEN

Elizabeth leaned back in the hackney coach and looked out of the window, watching the world go by. The novelty of the metropolis had not worn off during her long stay in London, and normally she spent much time marvelling at each new sight and landmark on her excursions about town. She watched idly now as the carriage passed several peddlers hawking their wares—travelling ink sellers, scissor grinders, fishmongers, flower girls, and other tradesmen—all shouting amidst the confusion of carriages and horses and carts and pedestrians hurrying through the streets.

Normally such a spectacle would have filled her with fascination. Today, however, she found that she was distracted. The discovery of Wickham's perfidy disturbed her greatly and she could not stop herself thinking about it. She reached into her reticule and pulled out the note that Darcy had returned to her, unfolding it again. She stared down at the hidden words that had been revealed and thought how ironic that such a letter, with every appearance of romantic beauty in its thick cream paper and ornamental scalloped edges, should have contained such a treacherous message.

As Elizabeth continued staring at the note, something began to nag at her. She chewed her bottom lip, thinking hard. Something bothered her...

She furrowed her brow and tried to think harder. Was it something she had heard? No, it was something she had seen... something about this beautiful letter to Mary King...

Elizabeth sat bolt upright.

Wickham's letter was written on paper with a distinctive curved scalloped edge... and she remembered now where she had seen a similar piece of paper.

In the hands of Georgiana Darcy.

The first time she had met Darcy's sister had been at that soirée held at Darcy House. After the singing and music display, she had walked over to join the girls by the pianoforte. They had been huddled together, giggling over something. She remembered them starting guiltily when she approached and Georgiana shoving something out of sight beneath the sheet music.

Then last night, at the Hursts' residence, she had walked into the music room and again found Georgiana and Amy huddled together in the corner. She had barely paid proper attention at the time, but now in her mind's eye, she saw the picture clearly: the two girls giggling, their heads bent together over something in Georgiana's hands...

The glimpse of cream paper protruding from her fingers...

The distinctive curved scalloped edge...

Elizabeth drew a sharp breath. Had Georgiana been receiving letters from Wickham too? Was that what the two girls had been giggling over all this time? Not mischievous schoolgirl notes, as she had imagined, but messages from a secret admirer?

She thought back suddenly to Georgiana's air of barely repressed excitement that morning and the way the girl had confessed to not sleeping a wink.

"To inspire so much love and admiration... it is beyond my wildest dreams! I had thought such sentiments only existed in romantic novels but then to discover that they could be real... and that I could excite them! Oh, it was the most exhilarating discovery!"

Georgiana must have been talking about the excitement of receiving such letters of love. The fervour of the girl's words worried Elizabeth. She had to make sure that Georgiana did not do anything reckless or indiscreet. She leaned forwards and called for the driver's attention, demanding that they turn back immediately.

"Eh?" The man looked at her incredulously.

"You must return to Darcy House at once!"

Elizabeth sat fretfully as the carriage turned and began retracing its route back to Grosvenor Square. When they pulled up in front of Darcy House at last, Elizabeth was alighting before the carriage had even come to a stop. She ran up the front steps and grabbed the brass knocker, not caring about decorum this time as she banged as hard as she could.

The door opened and Manning peered out, looking even more forbidding than he had this morning.

"Miss Bennet." He gave her a slight bow.

"Manning! Is Miss Darcy home?" asked Elizabeth breathlessly.

Manning looked her up and down before replying and Elizabeth knew that he was probably deploring her dishevelled appearance.

"I'm afraid the young mistress has gone out. Perhaps you would like to leave a message?" Clearly he had no intention of inviting her back into the house.

"Do you know where she has gone?" asked Elizabeth, hoping that her suspicions were unfounded. Georgiana might have simply gone out to call upon a family friend or perhaps even gone shopping again.

"I would not expect Miss Darcy to inform me of every detail of her planned excursions," said Manning pompously. "In any event, I consider it her private affair and would not feel at liberty to share such details with a casual acquaintance."

"Can you at least tell me if she was accompanied, perhaps by her maid?"

Something—some element of urgency in her expression—must have finally got through to the cantankerous butler. He regarded her silently for a moment, then relented.

"No, the mistress did not say, but... she was dressed in a riding habit and asked for her pony to be saddled."

"Was she in the habit of riding by herself?" asked Elizabeth in surprise.

Manning hesitated, then said, "No. I believe not. She is usually accompanied by the master or a groom."

Elizabeth felt her anxiety rising. "What about Mr Darcy? Is he at home? I must see him." She attempted to step into the house, hoping that Manning would step aside.

He remained stolidly in her path. "The

master has just left as well. For Cheapside."
The lines of disapproval deepened around his
mouth even more.

"Cheapside?" gasped Elizabeth. "Do you
know if he was going to the Gardiners'
residence?"

"The master did not say."

Elizabeth gritted her teeth in frustration.
She had thought that Darcy was taciturn, but
it was nothing compared to his butler! She
shifted from foot to foot, debating her next
move. She needed to speak to Darcy.
Georgiana *may* have gone on an innocent
excursion and she could have been worrying
for nothing, but until she was sure, she was
not willing to take the chance. Darcy was the
best person to ensure his sister's safety.

Elizabeth sighed. But if she were to return to
Cheapside now, she could miss him again as
he may have left by the time she arrived back
at her aunt and uncle's residence.

Oh, what a muddle!

"I will await Mr Darcy here," said Elizabeth
firmly, pushing suddenly past Manning. The
butler was taken off guard and he stumbled
back, letting her into the house. He spluttered
indignantly, but Elizabeth ignored him as she
marched down the hallway to the drawing
room.

"Please inform me as soon as your master or

mistress comes home," she called over her shoulder.

Once in the parlour, she did not sit down for she felt too restless. Instead, she paced up and down the room, pausing every so often to glance out the windows which overlooked Grosvenor Square. Fervently, she hoped that her suspicions were unfounded and that Georgiana would appear at any moment, having enjoyed a solitary jaunt on her pony and in danger of nothing more than a stern scolding from her brother.

But Georgiana did not appear. Gentlemen on horses trotted busily past, fashionably dressed ladies strolled slowly across the square, but no one approached the front entrance of Darcy House.

After a while, Elizabeth found herself wandering into the adjoining music room. Eager for some kind of distraction to occupy her anxious mind, she crossed to the pianoforte and began looking idly through the sheet music piled on top. Then her hands paused on the pages. She remembered that scene at the soirée once again: Georgiana and Amy had been standing in this very spot when she had come across them and Darcy's sister had hastily shoved something beneath these pages.

Wickham's letters?

Quickly, Elizabeth began flipping through sheets of music, searching for any sign of letters and notes. There was nothing. She looked through them twice more, shaking the sheaf of papers, turning each one over individually, wondering if she had somehow missed them.

But no. There was nothing.

Blowing a sigh of frustration, Elizabeth turned from the pianoforte. Then she paused and turned back, her gaze dropping to the piano stool.

Of course! The piano stool back in Longbourn featured a hinged seat which could be raised to reveal a compartment carved into the wood—a place to store sheet music, no doubt. She was sure that Georgiana's stool would be similar.

Elizabeth dropped to her knees beside the stool and gripped the edges of the padded seat, lifting it slowly. It raised up with a faint creak and Elizabeth found herself looking at a shallow compartment. There was another loose sheaf of music inside, but what really caught her eye was the bundle of letters tied with a pink ribbon.

Yes! Elizabeth grabbed them and stood up, fumbling as she tried to undo the ribbon. The letters fell out in a loose pile on the top of the instrument. She drew a sharp breath as she saw the large, bold "Wickham" at the bottom of each one, then cringed as she skimmed the contents—so similar to the letter he had written to Mary King: the same pretty avowals of love, the same seductive tone of admiration and longing. Elizabeth felt disgust rise like bile in her throat. What a smooth player Wickham was!

The sound of a step in the adjoining room roused Elizabeth from her thoughts and she looked up to see Darcy's tall figure in the doorway.

"Darcy!" she cried in relief, snatching up the letters and running across to him.

"Miss Bennet!" Darcy stared at her in surprise. "We were beginning to worry about you! I have just been to call upon your aunt and uncle, to share the news of Mary King's safe return, and I was extremely surprised to find that you had not returned. They were most concerned and thought—"

"Yes, I was on my way home, but I turned around and came back here," Elizabeth interrupted him. "I have something of far more import to tell you. You must find Georgiana at once!"

"Find her?" Darcy frowned. "Why, what is the matter?"

In answer, Elizabeth thrust the bundle of letters at him. "It is Wickham. He has been playing a double game. Mary King was not his only object. There is another young lady who has been victim of his seductive charm..." She raised worried eyes to his. "Your sister."

CHAPTER EIGHTEEN

"My sister?"

Darcy looked stunned for a moment, then he looked down at the letters he held in his hands. A look of such fury came over his face that Elizabeth took a step back hastily.

Darcy raised his head. His eyes were hard and bleak. "We must find them."

"But where? How?" said Elizabeth. She looked back down at the note that was dated the most recently. "This message here is almost identical to the one we intercepted, which he intended for Mary King..."

"Then he may be using the same ploy," said Darcy tersely. "When I was at the King residence, we deduced that Mary King would meet Wickham in Hyde Park. It is an ideal spot—it is near in distance and easily accessible for young ladies, without rousing too much suspicion, and large enough for a private meeting to go unnoticed in some discreet corner, concealed by foliage."

"Manning said that your sister was dressed in a riding habit..." Elizabeth remembered.

"Then she is likely to be heading for Hyde Park. That is the most popular place for hacking and where she would feel most comfortable and familiar." Darcy gave a frustrated shake of his head. "But Hyde Park is four hundred acres. It would be impossible to find her without some knowledge of where they are intending to meet."

"What about Miss King? Where did you locate her?"

"Along Ladies Mile, on the northern shore of the Serpentine. But there was no sign of Wickham and the more I think of it, the more I doubt that he would have chosen such an exposed meeting place. It seems that the choice was more due to Miss King's own desperate attempts to search for him."

Darcy turned and paced the room with jerky movements. His hands were clenched tight behind his back and Elizabeth could see a muscle ticking in his jaw. She felt a wave of compassion for him and had to resist the urge to reach out to him. Beneath that cold mask of control, Darcy must have been frantic. Aside from his concerns over his sister's personal safety in the hands of a ruthless man, he must have known that Georgiana's life could be completely ruined should this escapade become public. And this time, she was in London—a bigger city where it was much harder to locate a runaway and where far more people could discover the truth and gossip could circulate. It would be much harder to hush up a scandal here than it had been in Ramsgate. He had averted disaster once—only to have it return, ten times worse than before.

Elizabeth sighed and looked back down at the letters that Darcy had flung into the side table. Then she had a thought.

"Amy might know," she said, looking back up at Darcy.

He paused in his pacing. "Amy St John?"

Elizabeth nodded. "She and Miss Darcy are such dear friends—I think your sister might have confessed the whole scheme to her. Indeed, I saw them often huddled together, as if sharing a secret. That is how I came to suspect Georgiana's involvement with Wickham—I spied the two of them talking and laughing furtively over a note. I had thought it to be some innocent schoolgirl mischief, until I recalled seeing the scalloped edge to the paper, which was similar to the letter intended for Mary King."

Elizabeth thought back to that morning and added, "Amy came to visit earlier—and she was still here when I left. She was probably the last person to speak to Georgiana. She might have some idea of your sister's intentions."

She did not need to say more. Darcy was out of the house and across to the St John residence in a matter of minutes, with Elizabeth hard at his heels. A few moments later, they were shown into the neighbouring drawing room and Amy appeared, looking flustered.

"Where is Georgiana?" asked Darcy without preamble.

Amy's eyes widened. "What... What do you mean?"

"She has gone out and I believe that she may be in danger," said Darcy.

"I... I thought she went out riding," said Amy.

"In Hyde Park?"

Amy hesitated, then nodded.

"She is meeting someone there, is she not? Mr Wickham?" Elizabeth demanded.

Amy hesitated again, then dropped her eyes. "Yes," she whispered.

"Where?" said Darcy.

"I do not know," Amy said. "She did not tell me."

Darcy took a few steps towards the girl.

"Miss St John, it is imperative that we find Georgiana at once. Please try and think—did she say anything that might present a clue as to her intended destination?"

"I..." Amy's eyes darted nervously from one to the other. "I... I am not sure."

The girl's hesitation vexed Elizabeth. Did she not realise the urgency of the situation? Her friend could have been in real danger!

"Amy, you are not protecting Miss Darcy by covering up for her," she said earnestly. "Indeed, you could be consigning her to harm. If you know something, you must tell us."

"But... But Wickham will not harm her," protested Amy. "He loves her! He wrote her the most beautiful love letters... Oh, it is so romantic! I wish I could receive such letters, that I could inspire such passion in a man."

Elizabeth looked at her incredulously. How could the girl be so naive? "No gentleman who truly loved and respected a lady would behave the way Wickham has done," she said. "Were his intentions noble, he would have courted her openly, instead of engaging in such underhand communications. He has exposed Miss Darcy to censure and scandal, and to the possible ruination of her good name and her family's reputation."

Amy looked at her in horror. "You mean... you mean, Georgiana is lost forever? Oh no!"

She dissolved into tears, burying her face in her hands.

"She will not be lost if we can save her in time," said Elizabeth. "Cease your tears! Your weeping does no good. You need to get a hold of yourself and think. Think back to what Georgiana said to you this morning—perhaps there was a clue in something she said."

But Amy was not listening. She was hunched over, her face in her hands, crying inconsolably. Elizabeth sighed. She had little patience with tears and hysterics—perhaps due to the frequent histrionic behaviour indulged by her own mother and younger sisters at home.

She glanced at Darcy, expecting her exasperation to be mirrored in his face, but to her surprise, he stepped forwards and caught one of the girl's hands in his.

"Miss St John, pray do not distress yourself. We do not blame you for my sister's disappearance. It is natural that you should want to protect your friend. Come..." He led her to one of the sofas and gently assisted her into a seat. "Let me call a maid. Is there nothing you can take to give you present relief? A glass of wine—shall I get you one?"

Amy shook her head. Her face was still buried in her hands but her sobs was subsiding. Darcy sat down next to her and spoke soothingly. Elizabeth was amazed at his tender, patient manner with the girl.

At long last, Amy regained enough control to raise her face and look at them. Her eyes were red and puffy, her face tearstained, and she was taking deep, shuddering breaths, but she seemed to be calmer now.

She gave a little hiccup, then said, her voice quavering, "I... I do not remember Georgiana saying anything in particular about where she might be going. The only thing I can remember is her talking of meeting Wickham by the water."

"By the Serpentine?" asked Darcy.

Amy shook her head. "No... No, not the Serpentine. I know it is not that, for Georgiana said a small pool. By Rotten Row..." she added.

"A small pool by Rotten Row..." Darcy mused.

"But what other body of water can it be if not the Serpentine?" said Elizabeth, puzzled. "Though the lake is not beside Rotten Row and it is certainly not a 'small pool'. It makes no sense..."

"Georgiana spoke also of a valley," said Amy suddenly. "She said 'by the small pool in the valley, next to Rotten Row'." She looked at them hopefully. "Does that help with your deductions?"

Darcy said nothing, though his eyes were

thoughtful.

Then he sprang up suddenly. "'Small pool in the valley'...another word for a valley is a dell. There is a small area in Hyde Park called the Dell. It is at the east end of the Serpentine, just below the dam and accessed from Rotten Row by a short path. There is a little receiving pool, to catch the overflow from the Serpentine, down at the bottom of a short but steep slope. It is not a popular spot for it has been left to run wild. Indeed, the area is surrounded by trees and would be well concealed from the main paths. It would be an ideal meeting place for a secret assignation." Darcy nodded decisively. "That is where we should begin our search."

He turned back to Amy. "Thank you, Miss St John. Your assistance has been invaluable."

Amy sniffed and gave him a wobbly smile.

Darcy turned to Elizabeth. "Miss Bennet... I realise it may be presumptive of me to ask this, but will you accompany me to Hyde Park? My sister may be distressed by the turn of events and your presence would be comforting, as well as providing the necessary chaperonage to mitigate gossip. I would normally ask a female relative, but in this instance—"

"Of course," said Elizabeth quickly. "I should be glad to accompany you."

As she followed Darcy out of the house,

however, Elizabeth could not help wondering if they were too late...

CHAPTER NINETEEN

In a matter of minutes, they were on their way to Hyde Park in a light curricle drawn by a pair of well-matched bays. Darcy set a cracking pace, leaning forwards, his face intent, his hands working the reins expertly. Elizabeth clutched the side of the curricle as it sped through the cobbled London streets. She was not normally a nervous passenger, but the way Darcy was driving would have frightened even a member of the infamous Whip Club.

They careened around a corner and shot through the gates at Hype Park Corner. It was mid-afternoon and the rush had not started yet on Rotten Row. The wide bridle path was fairly empty and Darcy sent his horses tearing down the gravel-and-sand path. The Serpentine came into view on their right—a shimmering sheet of water, dotted with waterfowl, stretching towards a bridge in the distance. Darcy slowed the horses to a trot, then brought the curricle to a lurching stop beside the footpath. The horses stood, their chests heaving and their breaths puffing audibly as they tossed their manes.

"There." He jerked his head sideways.

Elizabeth followed his gaze to see a smaller path branching off from the main footpath alongside Rotten Row. It seemed to be leading off into a tangle of woods and shrubbery a short distance from the shores of the Serpentine.

Darcy flung down the reins and jumped up from the curricle, then came around and held his hand out for Elizabeth. She felt his hand grasp hers in a strong grip as he helped her down, then, to her surprise, he did not let it go as he started towards the side path. They hurried together towards the stand of trees and shrubbery, following the path and emerging at the top of a slope which dipped sharply down to a little valley. At the bottom of the valley lay a long, narrow pool, surrounded by a fringe of trees. It could almost have been pretty, were it not so wild and overgrown.

"Georgiana!" shouted Darcy, letting go of Elizabeth's hand as he began to run down the slope.

Elizabeth caught sight of what he had seen and gasped in alarm. Georgiana stood at the bottom of the slope, beside a tree next to the water. She was facing a tall young man, her hands held in both of his and her face raised invitingly as he leaned towards her...

"Georgiana!"

The young couple sprang apart and Georgiana looked up, her eyes widening in dismay as she saw Darcy. Wickham's eyes showed alarm too for a moment, then a calculating look came over his face. He stepped casually back and adopted a nonchalant stance as Darcy arrived in front of them, his eyes coldly furious.

"Fitzwilliam, it is not what you think—" protested Georgiana. "Wickham loves me! We knew you'd never understand, so we decided this was the best way. Once we're married—"

"You will never marry that fortune hunter," Darcy bit out. "I do not like to give you pain, Georgiana, but I must correct your assumption. This man does not love you. He is merely using you to further his own gain."

"No..." Georgiana shook her head, her face growing pale. "That is not true..."

"It is the whole truth. You must believe me, Georgiana." Darcy took a step towards his sister.

"No!" Georgiana shook her head wildly,

backing away from him. "You are wrong!

"Believe me in wishing nothing but your happiness," said Darcy desperately. "But in this regard, I must insist that you accept my judgement with regards to Wickham—"

"You are just treating me like a child again," cried Georgiana. "You do not give me credit for knowing my own mind! Wickham has been most candid with me from the start. He has told me of his most innermost thoughts and I have been—"

"Ask him about Mary King," said Darcy harshly.

A look of confusion crossed Georgiana's face. She turned to Wickham. "What... what does he mean?"

Wickham hesitated, then gave a careless shrug.

Darcy spoke up. "Mary King is another young lady whom Wickham has been attempting to seduce. Like you, she received numerous letters, each with a hidden message written in invisible ink. I have seen one of these letters and it is almost identical to the message he sent you. A message filled with false declarations of love, written with one motive— to coerce you into an elopement and enable Wickham to gain access to your fortune."

Georgiana was still shaking her head, but it was a weak gesture of denial as she attempted to reject her brother's accusations. One look at Wickham's smug expression told her that Darcy spoke the truth. Wickham was not even bothering to argue or deny it. Georgiana raised her hands to her mouth, her eyes wide and stricken. She gave a choked cry. Elizabeth went up to the girl and put an arm around her.

"Shh..." she said softly, rubbing the girl's back. "I am sorry, Miss Darcy, but at least you are safe now."

"I see you have discovered my schemes," said Wickham with a smirk. "But do not wallow too much in your triumph yet." He swaggered up to Darcy. "I am sure you would not want this story spread across London. Just imagine! Georgiana Darcy engaged in an intrigue involving secret letters and running off to meet her lover in the park. The gossips will have a field day. Your sister's life will be ruined forever. " He laughed nastily, ignoring Georgiana's whimper of distress.

"What do you want?" asked Darcy through clenched teeth.

Wickham gave a slow smile. "Well, since you have cost me the opportunity of gaining a fortune, you will have to compensate me for that. Let me see... shall we say ten thousand pounds?" He gave Darcy an insolent pat on the arm. "I am sure you would be willing to pay that to ensure your precious sister's reputation remains unsullied. Otherwise, I may have to consider selling a story to the newspapers..."

Darcy's hands clenched reflexively and, for a moment, Elizabeth thought that he was going to hit Wickham. White lines of anger showed around his mouth and his dark eyes were smouldering.

But she knew that Darcy understood he could not afford to cause a scene. Already they could hear the distant sounds of carriages and riders arriving in Hyde Park for the "fashionable hour". Any disturbance here, so close to Rotten Row, would be quickly discovered and the ensuing gossip and scandal would be even more damaging to Georgiana's future. The priority now was to resolve the situation as quietly as possible and return Georgiana to the sanctity of her home, where she was safe from the threat of malicious conjecture.

Wickham gave another nasty laugh. "I am sure you see my point. Do not think that I would not carry out my threat. Your sister will be humiliated and censured by all of society if you do not comply with my demands."

Darcy stiffened but said nothing.

Wickham smiled, showing his teeth. "I shall come by Darcy House tomorrow and collect my due. Until then... as the French say: *au revoir*!" He swept them a jaunty little bow, then turned and sauntered out of the dell.

There was a long moment of silence after he left. Darcy looked down and exhaled slowly. Elizabeth could see that his shoulders were still rigid with tension, but he unclenched his fists and turned slowly back to them.

"Oh, Fitzwilliam... I-I am so sorry!" Georgiana burst into tears, flinging herself into his arms.

Darcy sighed and patted his sister's back, whilst she sobbed into his chest. He raised his head and his eyes met Elizabeth's.

"To think that I have to accede to Wickham's requests..." he said bitterly.

Elizabeth shared his anguish. "Is there no other way? It is not right that Wickham should remain unpunished—and now even rewarded!"

Darcy's lips tightened. "There is no other means to protect Georgiana from his exploitation. I am obliged to fulfil his demands—"

"Wait," said Elizabeth suddenly. She stepped forwards excitedly. "I have an idea."

CHAPTER TWENTY

Wickham arrived at Darcy House the following day at three o'clock in the afternoon. He walked into the foyer with a cheerful swagger and whistled as he looked around him.

"Fancy place, eh?"

Manning looked at him sourly. "Mr Darcy is awaiting you in his study."

"Well... mustn't keep him waiting then, must we?" Wickham smirked, turning to follow Manning down the hallway.

He stepped into the study and found Darcy standing looking out of the window, with his hands clasped behind his back. Wickham grinned to himself as he saw the rigid set of Darcy's shoulders.

"Mr Wickham, sir," Manning intoned.

Darcy turned. His face seemed to be set in stone as he indicated a seat in front of his desk, then sat down himself.

Wickham sank into one of the upholstered chairs and said to Manning, "Bring me a brandy, will you, my man?"

Manning's face turned purple. He looked at Darcy, who gave a curt nod. The butler hesitated, then stalked from the room. He returned a few moments later with a glass of the best Armagnac brandy. Wickham took it and stuck his nose into the glass, sniffing appreciatively as he swirled the amber liquid around.

"Ah... only the best for Fitzwilliam Darcy. I should have known." He laughed and tossed the drink back in one swallow, then wiped his mouth and handed the empty glass back to an indignant Manning. "One more, I think."

"I think Mr Wickham has had enough refreshment for the time being," said Darcy crisply. "You may go, Manning."

"Very good, sir." The butler scowled at Wickham, then turned and stalked out of the study.

"Just like old times, eh, Darcy?" said Wickham with a snide laugh. "I seem to remember a similar interview several years ago—you all high and mighty behind your desk, me sitting on this side—and how you grilled me for a measly three thousand pounds!" He raised mocking eyebrows. "A most uncharitable attitude when providing a gift, wouldn't you say?"

"That was not a gift," Darcy grated. "It was payment in lieu of the living which you yourself refused to undertake and which you were amply compensated for."

"Now, now, Darcy, let's not get bogged down with details," said Wickham with a malicious laugh. "Gifts, legacies, payments in lieu... it all amounts to the same thing, doesn't it? Your father—*my godfather*—was excessively attached to me and wanted nothing more than to provide amply for me. After all, he was one of the best men that ever breathed and the truest friend I ever had—"

"Do not *speak* of my father," Darcy growled, his hands clenching on his desk.

Wickham raised his eyebrows. "Oooh... temper, Darcy. You were always prone to losing it with me, even when we were boys. I remember the last time we faced each other thus, you lost guard on your temper as well..." He gave a taunting smile. "Indeed, you warned me never to approach you again for further funds... and now here I am... and you are about to pay me more than double!" He laughed delightedly.

Darcy took a deep breath and unclenched

his fists. "Why don't we get on with it, then?"

Wickham stopped laughing and leaned forwards, suddenly serious. "Yes. Time to get down to business. Do you have the bank cheque for the amount I requested?"

Darcy pulled open a drawer and withdrew a narrow slip of paper. He waved this slowly and Wickham's eyes followed the movement of the paper greedily.

"Right here."

Wickham reached for the cheque, but Darcy pulled his hand back. "Just a moment."

Wickham narrowed his eyes. "What?"

"I have spoken to my solicitor and he has advised me that in order to prevent further blackmail attempts on your part, I must obtain an agreement from you."

"What agreement?" asked Wickham suspiciously.

Darcy pulled a second sheet of paper out of the drawer and laid it on the desk. "A signed agreement guaranteeing your silence on the subject of my sister in the future."

"I am not signing anything," snapped Wickham.

Darcy sat back, putting the cheque back in the drawer. "In that case, there is nothing more to discuss."

"Wait." Wickham scowled and held out his hand. "Let me see the agreement."

Darcy pushed the sheet of paper towards him. Wickham picked it up and scanned it, then his eyes narrowed.

"It says here: 'I hereby admit my guilt in attempting to seduce...'." He shot Darcy a smug smile. "Thought you could catch me on that one, huh? I am not signing anything where I admit my guilt." He put the paper down and jabbed a finger on it. "You cross that line out."

Darcy's mouth tightened and he hesitated, then he reached forwards and pulled the paper towards him. As Wickham watched gleefully, he dipped his quill in the inkwell and scratched out that phrase, then initialled the change. He pushed it back to Wickham.

"There. Does that meet with your satisfaction?"

Wickham picked the paper up again and read the words. "Mm... Yes, I suppose this will do."

"So you will sign?" Darcy held the quill up towards him.

Wickham gave him another suspicious look. "Let me read it again." He was silent as he went slowly over the words on the paper:

I, George Wickham, hereby relinquish all

claims to further compensation from Fitzwilliam Darcy

I will refrain from any public exposure of my involvement with Georgiana Darcy

I declare that I am of sound mind and body, and not acting under duress or undue influence,

George Wickham Esq.

He hesitated a moment longer, then took the quill from Darcy's fingers and signed his name with flourish at the bottom. "There." He tossed the quill down, shoved the paper across the desk to Darcy, and held out his hand. "And now the money."

Darcy handed over the cheque. "How did you know I would keep my word? You signed the agreement first. I could have refused to give you the cheque once the agreement was in my possession."

Wickham gave a sneering laugh. "I know you, Darcy. Strait-laced and proper as they come. You would never break your word as a gentleman." He leaned forwards. "See, that's the difference between you and me. You could never be as ruthless as I am to achieve my goals."

He pocketed the cheque and stood up, giving Darcy a flamboyant bow. "Much obliged, sir. And now, I must take my leave."

Darcy rolled up the agreement, then crossed the room and quietly opened the door of the study.

"After you."

Wickham swaggered out, and a moment later Darcy followed him and accompanied him down the hallway. As they reached the foyer, Manning stepped forwards and said:

"Shall I call for a hackney coach, sir?"

"Hmm... exemplary service, Darcy," said Wickham with a mocking smile. "You have your staff well trained." He turned to Manning and said, "Yes, my man. I wish to have transport to my lodgings."

"Very good, sir." Manning turned to the side table next to him and picked up a dinner gong. He struck it hard and the noise reverberated loudly in the foyer.

Wickham frowned. "What's this—a joke?"

"No, not a joke," said Manning calmly. "Transport to your lodgings. Your *new* lodgings, that is."

The next moment, all the doors leading into the foyer were flung open and several officers of the regiment marched in.

"Hey!" said Wickham angrily as they grabbed his arms. "Release me!"

"We are here to provide you with an escort to your ship," one of the officers said, his face impassive.

"My... my ship?" Wickham gaped at them. "What the hell are you talking about?" He tried to wrench his arm out of their grasp, but did not succeed. "LET GO OF ME!"

Darcy stepped forwards, a cool smile on his lips. "It will be more pleasant for you if you do not resist."

Wickham glared at Darcy. "You cannot do this! I have committed no crime! You have no right to detain me!"

Darcy raised an eyebrow. "Are you sure? That is not what this piece of paper says." He held up the signed agreement.

Wickham narrowed his eyes. "I never signed my rights away. And I certainly never confessed to any crime! I read that agreement from top to bottom and I know exactly what I signed for!"

Darcy's eyebrows climbed higher. "Perhaps your memory needs refreshing."

He unrolled the agreement slowly and held the paper up in front of Wickham's face. The other man stared at the paper—at the extra words which had somehow magically appeared between the previous lines:

I, George Wickham, hereby relinquish all
my rights as a free member of the British empire and
claims to further compensation from Fitzwilliam Darcy
as befits my punishment for my crimes.
I will refrain from any public exposure of my involvement with Georgiana Darcy
and admit that all claims of seduction or elopement are a complete fabrication.
I declare that I am of sound mind and body, and not acting under duress or undue influence,
as I state my wish to enter into voluntary exile in exchange for transportation to Australia.

George Wickham Esq.

Wickham's face drained of all colour. "But... but..."

"This is your signature, is it not?" said Darcy, pointing to the bottom of the page.

"Yes, but I never agreed to those things!" Wickham snarled. "You bastard! You tricked me! You had those lines written in invisible ink—and then revealed them after I signed the agreement—"

"Come, come, Mr Wickham," said Darcy with a laugh. "Invisible ink? I think you have been reading too many novels. I assure you, these words were on the paper when you signed it. You did say you read the agreement from top and bottom and knew exactly what you signed for... did you not?"

"I... I... " Wickham spluttered, at a loss for words for the first time in his life.

Darcy handed the agreement to one of the officers. "Good. Then we are in accord. All that remains is to wish you a pleasant journey."

Wickham's eyes bulged and he began to struggle violently. "Wait! You can't... STOP! You can't do this! I never said... you can't transport me to Australia! Darcy! You are condemning me to the life of a convict in a penal colony! You are a gentleman and a man of honour! You can't do this—"

"Ah, that is where you are wrong." Darcy stepped close to him and said, his voice dangerously quiet, "You see, Wickham, we are much more alike than you think. I too can be ruthless in order to achieve my goals." He stepped back and nodded to the officers. "Take him away."

"No! *NO!* Wait...!"

Wickham was almost hysterical, fighting savagely now for his freedom, but he was no match for the four officers as they bore him out of the front door and into the waiting carriage.

Manning shut the front door with a resounding thud as the sound of the carriage faded away. Then he turned to Darcy and bestowed one of his rare smiles.

"If I may say so, sir, the invisible ink was a masterstroke of genius."

"Ah, do not compliment me, Manning," said Darcy with a smile. "The credit belongs to Miss Elizabeth Bennet. It was her idea to play Wickham at his own game and use his own trickery to condemn him."

Manning raised his eyebrows and a look of grudging respect came into his eyes. "I had not expected such resourcefulness from Miss Bennet."

Darcy laughed. "In time, Manning, I think you too will grow the share my admiration for that pert mind and spirited temper"

CHAPTER TWENTY-ONE

Elizabeth sighed as she shifted on the sofa. The whole evening had seemed to drag and now she heartily wished that their guests would leave so that she could retire to bed. She felt a stab of guilt at the thought. It was rare for her aunt and uncle to entertain—and they were giving this evening party in honour of their nieces—so she should not have been ungrateful. She just could not understand why she felt so listless all evening, finding the conversation boring and the company dull.

No, she was lying to herself. She *did* know why. It was because Darcy was not here. She had been taken aback and disappointed when Bingley had arrived without his friend; she had been expecting Darcy, anticipating his arrival with something almost like excitement...

But he had not come.

She wondered why, but she dared not ask Bingley, for fear of giving the wrong impression. After all, it was not as if she was interested in Darcy himself, of course. She was simply hoping to hear the details of the encounter with Wickham. She knew that Wickham would have gone to Darcy House this morning and Darcy would have put their plan into action. She had been looking forward to hearing the details of the encounter from him this evening.

She heaved another sigh and stood up, impatient with herself. Well, Darcy hadn't come and that was that. No doubt he would send her a message tomorrow to inform her of the outcome of the subterfuge. In the meantime, she had to stop herself dwelling on that provocative gentleman!

Elizabeth scanned the room, looking for a distraction, and realised suddenly that Jane was nowhere to be seen. Puzzled, she hurried to her aunt's side.

"Where is Jane?" she whispered.

Mrs Gardiner gave a complacent smile. "I saw her and Mr Bingley slip out a few moments ago. I believe they are in your uncle's study."

"Is that quite appropriate?"

Mrs Gardner reached out and gave Elizabeth's hand a squeeze. "My dear, I do not think Mr Bingley's intentions towards Jane are dishonourable. And I feel that this is one time when it may be very beneficial to give them some privacy. There may be matters they wish to discuss—questions which may need to be answered," she said with a meaningful look.

Elizabeth raised her eyebrows. "Oh! You think Mr Bingley is about to propose to Jane—?"

"Hush!" said her aunt quickly. "I am not certain, but I have an inkling. While I do not share your mother's passionate pursuit of the matrimonial state for her daughters, I am pleased to do what I can to facilitate a happy union, if it is in my power."

Elizabeth looked around again. No one else seemed to have noticed Jane and Bingley's absence. Nevertheless, she felt slightly uneasy. "Perhaps I should go and check on them—"

"Leave it be, Lizzy," Mrs Gardner advised. "I am confident that it shall be for the best."

"But I—"

Elizabeth broke off as she saw Bingley and Jane re-enter the drawing room and quietly joined the group by the tea service. She could see that Jane's face was glowing with happiness. She longed to rush over to her sister's side and ask her what had occurred, but she restrained herself.

When they were finally alone in their shared

bedroom, Elizabeth looked eagerly at her sister. "I saw you and Mr Bingley disappear from the drawing room for a few moments this evening—"

"Oh Lizzy—he loves me! And he wants to marry me!" Jane burst out, embracing Elizabeth.

Elizabeth gave her sister a squeeze. "Jane, I am so delighted for you! There are none so deserving and I am sure that Mr Bingley will make you very happy."

"He is riding to Longbourn tomorrow morning to ask Papa for his permission—but I must write to Mama myself as well and inform her. Oh Lizzy, to know that what I have to relate will give such pleasure to all my dear family. I am the happiest creature in the world!"

The sisters had much to say and they talked long into the night. And the next day brought another happy surprise, for when Bingley returned from Hertfordshire that evening, he brought Mr and Mrs Bennet with him. The latter could not contain her raptures at the engagement and was too impatient to wait until her daughters' return home. She arrived at the Gardiners' babbling excitedly about wedding gowns and special licences.

"Oh, my dear, dear Jane—I am so happy!"

she gushed. "I knew how it would be. I was sure you could not be so beautiful for nothing! I remember, as soon as I saw Mr Bingley when he first came to Hertfordshire last year, I thought how likely it was that you should come together. Oh, he is the handsomest young man I have ever seen... and five thousand a year... and very likely more!"

The younger Bennet girls had sent notes congratulating their eldest sister and petitioning her for objects of happiness which she might be able to dispense in the future. Mary asked for the use of the library at Netherfield, whilst Kitty and Lydia begged for regular balls to be held there.

There was one other letter that had also come from Longbourn with their mother and father, which held news of interest, particularly to Elizabeth. Mr Bennet shared it with them at breakfast the following morning. It was a missive from Mr Collins and amongst his usual rambling sentences of pompous nothings, there was an item of note. He mentioned that his patroness, Lady Catherine de Bourgh, was particularly displeased with a rumour which was circulating about London.

"The subject of the gossip is her nephew, Mr Darcy; it appears that he has expressed the likelihood of marrying soon and that the lady he would choose is of an inferior family, from a

small country town," Mr Bennet read aloud.

Elizabeth felt her heart give a lurch. Darcy getting married?

"*Lady Catherine is appalled at the impropriety of such a match*," Mr Bennet continued reading. "*She has made it clear, with her usual condescension, that she will never give her blessing to such a disgraceful union.*" Mr Bennet looked up and raised his eyebrows. "I hardly think her ladyship's displeasure will make much difference in this instance. I had not the impression from Mr Darcy that he is a man who cares overmuch about pleasing others. He certainly does not need his aunt's consent—or her blessing—for his marriage and he seems a man who is determined to have his way."

Elizabeth swallowed uncomfortably. The news upset her more than she liked to admit. Darcy marrying an unknown country girl? Her thoughts flew to Amy St John and she remembered the warm looks he had bestowed on the girl, the many times he had gallantly gone to her rescue, the tender patience he had shown her, even in the midst of worry about Georgiana...

Perhaps those actions had not stemmed from kind chivalry, as she had thought, but from genuine affection and attraction for the girl.

Mr Bennet noticed her discomposure. "Lizzy, you look as if you did not enjoy this correspondence. I would have thought that such dramas should amuse you greatly."

"Oh... I am excessively diverted," said Elizabeth quickly.

"I wonder who his chosen bride can be?" said Mrs Bennet. "She has made a most triumphant match, to be sure! Mr Darcy may be a disagreeable man, but did you know that he has *ten* thousand a year? And a house in town... and the most magnificent estate in Derbyshire." She turned to Jane. "Mr Darcy was at dinner with you several times in the past week, was he not? Did he give any indication of his upcoming engagement?"

Jane shook her head. "No, Mr Darcy does not speak much in general. Though..." She paused thoughtfully. "At the last dinner we had together, he did seem particularly animated whilst he was conversing with Miss St John. She is a dear friend of Darcy's sister and she is certainly of humble country origins. Her father is a clergyman, I believe."

"So Mr Darcy was paying her particular attention, was he?" asked Mrs Bennet with nosy interest.

"He has always been extremely kind to her. I do not know if I have ever discerned a particular affection for her, though he did dance with her and no one else at Lady Grantley's ball."

"And what sort of girl is Miss St John?"

"She's a very nice sort of girl," said Jane. "Though perhaps a trifle shy. She is a great friend of Miss Darcy's and the two of them appear to get on famously."

"Well, then perhaps she would make an admirable sister—should she marry the brother,"

Elizabeth felt a jab of pain in her heart as she listened to the conversation. Was Mr Darcy really to marry Amy? It would undoubtedly be a good match on her side—and she was sure that Darcy would treat the girl with kindness. Indeed, why should he not treat her with tenderness and love? After all, he must be in love with the girl. Why else would he be challenging the expectations of duty and society by marrying her?

The topic of conversation had moved on now to Jane's wedding arrangements and Elizabeth attempted to listen with interest, although she found it hard to concentrate. Her appetite seemed to have deserted her as well and she toyed listlessly with a warm roll on her plate. Her thoughts kept returning to Mr Darcy being in love with Amy St John and she wondered why the notion should make her feel so miserable.

CHAPTER TWENTY-TWO

For the rest of the day, the thought of Darcy's imminent engagement occupied Elizabeth's mind completely. She struggled with a terrible sense of loss and was confused by her unhappy feelings. To make things worse, she had no word from Darcy—not even a note to inform her of Wickham's successful disposal. She wondered suddenly if he had forgotten her, now that the danger was dispelled and her usefulness gone. The thought brought her almost as much pain as the alternative of Darcy being too preoccupied by Amy St John to spare her any thought.

Jane noticed her low spirits and remarked upon it when they were alone together that evening.

"Lizzy... is aught the matter? You have not

been your usual lively self."

Elizabeth shrugged and attempted a bright smile. "I am sorry, my dear Jane. I do not mean to put a damper on your happiness. Indeed, I am looking forward to the engagement luncheon tomorrow." She hesitated, then said, "I am perhaps a trifle fatigued. I have enjoyed our visit with Aunt and Uncle immensely but I am looking forward now to the peace and quiet of Longbourn. Perhaps I am just tired of London society."

Jane looked at her for a long moment, then said hesitantly, "I do not mean to pry, Lizzy— and I shall certainly desist from asking should you prefer me to drop the subject—but I noticed that your low spirits seemed to come on this morning. In fact, since the reading of Mr Collins's letter and the revelation that Mr Darcy is soon to be wed."

Elizabeth coloured. Her sister knew her too well. "The news was a surprise," she admitted.

"But why should it upset you so? I know how much you dislike him."

Elizabeth shifted uncomfortably, wishing now that she had perhaps been more circumspect in her previous criticisms of Mr Darcy.

Jane looked at Elizabeth thoughtfully. "Lizzy... Do you think you might have formed a *tendre* for Mr Darcy?"

"I..." Elizabeth paused, suddenly unsure how to reply. Was Jane right? Was that why she felt the way she did? Has she really fallen in love with Mr Darcy?

The revelation filled her with a mixture of dismay and elation. She realised what a fool she had been. How could she have thought that she disliked him all this time? She saw now that Darcy was exactly the man who, in disposition and talents, would most suit her. Their temperaments—though distinctly different—would complement and enhance each other's—by her liveliness, his mind might have been softened, his manners improved, and from his judgement, information, and knowledge of the world, she would have received great benefit.

And much more than that, he would have made her *happy*. She understood now that Mr Darcy was the one man she could respect and admire—and give her heart to completely. Was it not the most terrible irony that when she could no longer have any hope of receiving his regard, she should desperately long for it?

Elizabeth carried her miserable thoughts with her to Darcy House the next day, where a small luncheon party was being held to celebrate Bingley and Jane's engagement. The celebration should really have been hosted by one of Bingley's sisters at the Hursts' residence, but both Caroline and Louisa had been so displeased and mortified by their brother's choice of bride that they had been loath to offer any hospitality.

Bingley was pleasantly surprised, however, when his friend, Darcy, stepped into the breach, offering to host the function at Darcy House instead. Recalling his friend's stern warnings about the imprudence of such a match, Bingley was surprised now to find Darcy supporting a celebration. But being of a cheerful, easy temper, he did not dwell overmuch on the subject, and accepted his friend's offer with simple gratitude. Caroline Bingley and Mrs Hurst had grudgingly accepted the invitation and decided that the opportunity to enjoy the gracious surrounds of Darcy House would mitigate the insult of having to spend more time with the Bennetts and the Gardiners.

Jane was naturally the centre of attention and Elizabeth was glad to stay at the back of their party as they were welcomed by Darcy into his home.

"I must apologise for my sister's absence," said Darcy gravely as he escorted them into the drawing room. "She has been unwell and is still recovering. She will be unable to join us today and she sends her regrets."

"Oh, we are very sorry to hear that," said Jane, her eyes full of concern. "I hope it is nothing serious?"

Darcy's eyes met Elizabeth's briefly, then he looked back at Jane. "I am sure, with the passage of time, she will soon recover." He smiled. "But let us not dwell on that today. This event is to celebrate your engagement. Congratulations, Miss Bennet. I believe you have made my friend a very happy man," he said warmly.

"La... but we hear that you will soon be following in your friend's footsteps, sir?" said Mrs Bennet, giving Mr Darcy an arch smile and speaking with a familiarity which made Elizabeth cringe. She knew that her mother loved to gossip and was no doubt hoping to delve deeper into Darcy's rumoured engagement.

"Mama!" she hissed. "That is Mr Darcy's private affair."

Darcy's eyes met hers again and there was an expression in them that she could not quite fathom. He turned back to Mrs Bennet and said coolly, "I think your daughter's engagement to Mr Bingley should be all that concerns us today. One ought not to steal the thunder from their happy moment."

It was a far more courteous set-down than

her mother deserved and Elizabeth was both surprised and grateful. She was glad when they all moved into the drawing room, though she continued to be anxious about Mrs Bennet's behaviour. She flushed as she saw Bingley's sisters turn away from her mother in contempt. Elizabeth's mood was not improved when she was approached by Amy St John. The other girl seemed to be brimming with excitement and drew her aside to whisper excitedly:

"Miss Bennet... I hope you will forgive my presumption but I feel that I *must* share the news with you! I know that you would share in my happiness."

"But of course, Miss St John, though I confess I do not know what you are speaking of?"

"Oh, please call me Amy! And I speak of my engagement!" She beamed.

"Oh... I see... er, congratulations," said Elizabeth. Her lips felt stiff as she attempted to smile. "That is wonderful news."

"Indeed, I did not even think that he could love me! With his position and wealth, the thought that he would notice a little nobody like me is beyond comprehension. And yet, ever since the dance at Lady Grantley's ball, I have been flattered to receive such tender attentions from him... that I began to hope..." She gripped

Elizabeth's hand, her eyes sparkling. "And yesterday, he made me the happiest of women by asking for my hand! If it wasn't for Georgiana and my friendship with her, this would have never happened."

She glanced over her shoulder with a tender smile. Elizabeth followed her gaze and saw Darcy standing next to Bingley, conversing with her aunt and uncle. She felt as if a vise was clamped around her heart, squeezing it painfully.

But she kept the smile resolutely on her face and said to Amy, "I am very happy for you. I am sure that you deserve his affections and it is most worthy of him to look beyond the superficial values of wealth and social position."

"Yes, well, there will be those who disapprove," said Amy, her face sobering. "That is why we have not yet made it official. He intends to approach my father first, before announcing it in the papers. I know there will be many who will be horrified at the thought such a great family accepting me as a daughter-in-law. I know I may be censured and despised." She smiled. "But I do not fear. I know that our love shall prevail. Oh, Miss Bennet—to think that I was facing the bleak prospect of life as a poor drudge in a seminary... and now instead, I shall be a lady of great consequence!"

"It is a most happy outcome," said Elizabeth as sincerely as she could. "I... I shall look forward to reading the announcement in the papers."

Feeling unable to face the girl's happiness any longer—and ashamed at her own weakness—Elizabeth excused herself. She hesitated, however, as she looked at the other guests. The luncheon was being served buffet style, with a selection of cold meats, salads, fish, game pies, pastries, and cakes laid out on the sideboard. Most of the guests were congregated around the food, admiring the dishes and helping themselves to the gourmet delicacies, whilst the rest had taken their heaped plates and were sitting in small groups around the large drawing room.

Elizabeth could not bring herself to join them. Her feelings were too tumultuous, her thoughts too disturbed. She slipped out of the drawing room and wandered down the hallway back towards the main foyer. Manning was nowhere to be seen but there was a set of doors on the other side of the staircase which was slightly ajar. She caught a glimpse of sunlight and the flash of greenery. Those doors must have led to the gardens.

Elizabeth hesitated. She could always plead a headache, she decided, and right now the temptation of a little quiet solitude was overwhelming. She made a decision and pushed the door fully open, stepping out into the fresh air.

CHAPTER TWENTY-THREE

Darcy had noticed Elizabeth slipping away. Indeed, he could hardly help noticing everything she did. When she was in the room, she drew his eyes like a magnet, and he found himself admiring every nuance of her expressions, every look, every gesture. He had immediately noticed that she seemed in low spirits when she arrived today. The sparkle was gone from her fine brown eyes and the teasing laughter from her lips. What had happened to grieve her so?

He had watched her surreptitiously from across the room, seeing the way her shoulders had slumped as she talked with Amy St John. It had taken all his self-control to resist the urge to hurry across the room to her, to comfort and soothe her.

Not that she would necessarily appreciate my attentions, Darcy reminded himself. He had been gratified that she had come to him for help in dealing with the note for Miss King, and he had felt a closeness to her when they had worked together to save Georgiana, but was that an indication that she might possess tender feelings for him? Darcy was almost afraid to let himself hope.

And now the sight of Elizabeth in misery tore at his heart. Darcy saw her leave and followed her quietly out of the room. The hallway was empty but the sight of the open doors to the courtyard gardens gave him a clue as to her whereabouts. He stepped outside and followed the flagstone pathway around the house to the walled garden at the side of the property. The sound of birdsong drifted down from the trees and the soft tinkle of water from the fountain filled the air.

He saw Elizabeth immediately. She was sitting on the bench beneath the mulberry tree, gazing into the distance, her face sad and forlorn. The sound of his steps on the stone path made her jerk around and she sprang up as she saw him.

"Mr Darcy—"

"Please..." He held a hand up. "I have no wish to disturb your pleasant solitude. I was merely concerned as to your welfare. I noticed you leave the drawing room..."

"Ah... yes... I... I had a headache," said Elizabeth. "I thought perhaps some fresh air might provide a curative for it."

They stood facing each other and an awkward silence descended between them. At last, Darcy cleared his throat and said:

"I am sorry I have not been able to call at Gracechurch Street to apprise you of the outcome with Wickham. The shock of his betrayal hit Georgiana hard. I thought she rallied at first but after Wickham was removed by the authorities she became feverish and distressed. I have been occupied with her care—she was so ill that I did not like to leave her side."

"Oh, I am sorry..." cried Elizabeth. "Is she better now?"

Darcy inclined his head. "She will recover. She will never be the same carefree young girl she once was... but perhaps those are the steps one is obliged to take on the road to adulthood." He sighed.

"I am sorry," Elizabeth murmured again. "Please pass on my best wishes to Miss Darcy and let me know if there is anything I can do to help."

Darcy smiled at her. "I shall. And do not worry. She is much better already. Furthermore, thanks to you, at least I am secure in the knowledge that Wickham can never harm her again."

Elizabeth looked at him with a tentative smile. "So the plan worked?"

"Beautifully. Your idea with the invisible ink was—as Manning put it—a masterstroke of genius," said Darcy with a chuckle.

Elizabeth blushed. They lapsed into silence again. Elizabeth seemed to be grappling with something—twice she opened her mouth as if to say something, only to shut it again.

"Miss Bennet... is there something you wish to say?" asked Darcy.

"I..." She hesitated, then took a deep breath and said quickly, "I must apologise for my mother's impertinence earlier in enquiring about your forthcoming marriage. I fully understand why you would not wish to speak of such a private matter. However, I would like to take this opportunity to wish you every happiness."

Darcy's brows drew together. "I beg your pardon?"

Elizabeth looked at him in confusion. "For your wedding... with Miss St John."

"I am not marrying Miss St John."

"But..." Elizabeth looked at him desperately. "But the rumours... and Mr Collins said that Lady Catherine..."

"I should hardly think you the type to give

credence to rumours, Miss Bennet," he said with a teasing smile.

Elizabeth looked even more confused. "But... Amy herself told me..."

"What did Miss St John tell you?"

"That she was engaged to be married," Elizabeth whispered. "To a gentleman of great wealth and consequence."

"That may be true but that gentleman is not me. I have a feeling it is Lord Denning, the young Earl of Shrewsbury, who was much taken with Miss St John at Lady Grantley's ball."

"Oh!"

Darcy gazed down at Elizabeth. He could see a mixture of emotions chase each other across her face. She looked as if a huge weight had been lifted off her shoulders. Her eyes were bright with sudden joy, and he felt a surge of hope, such as he had never felt before.

He stepped closer, so that they were almost touching, and reached out to grasp her hand. Her eyes widened but she did not resist.

Darcy said softly, "If Miss St John *had* been engaged to me... would you have cared?"

Elizabeth dropped her eyes. "Yes," she whispered, unable to look at him.

"Why?" he asked, his heart pounding suddenly with hope.

"Because..." Elizabeth licked her lips.

"Because I would have... lost you."

Darcy drew a sharp intake of breath. He raised her hand slowly to her lips and pressed a soft kiss to her fingers.

"You could never lose me, my darling, because I love you."

"Oh..." Elizabeth stared up at him in wonder.

"Do you think... you could love me too?"

Happiness suffused her face. "I do! I do love you too," she whispered.

Darcy pulled her into his arms and his lips came down on hers. The birds twittered softly above their heads as they clung together, their hearts beating fast, their bodies melding as their mouths drank in their first tentative taste of each other. At last, Darcy raised his head and released her.

He shook his head and chuckled. "From that first time I saw you across the assembly room in Meryton, you have captivated me with your wit, charm, and beauty—"

"Nay, sir," Elizabeth said, her face breaking into a smile. "My beauty you had early withstood, as I well remember overhearing you say during the assembly ball when we first met. I was not even tolerable enough to tempt you."

Darcy looked shamefaced. "That was abominable of me. I should never have said such uncharitable words. I think it was merely a desperate protest for I knew, in my heart, that I was already under your spell. But I resisted... oh, how I resisted!" He gave a shake of his head, laughing wryly.

"I too," admitted Elizabeth. "I spent so much time telling myself how disagreeable you were and how much I disliked your company... until I almost believed it!"

"We have both been fools," said Darcy. "But no longer. We shall go back in now and I shall waste no time in asking your father's permission for your hand. And we shall be married by special licence! How should you like to have a double wedding with Jane, my love?" He smiled down at her.

"I should like that above all else," said Elizabeth, her eyes shining.

"Then it shall be done," said Darcy softly as he leaned down towards her.

He brushed his lips tenderly against hers, then pulled her close and kissed her more fully. He felt Elizabeth's arms creep up around his neck and revelled in the feeling of holding her close to him.

They broke apart at last, both more than a little breathless, and Elizabeth gave a dry laugh.

"The rumour-mongers shall be pleased, for they will be proven right. You *are* marrying a girl of unknown family, from unfashionable country society, and probably shocking many in society with your choice," she teased.

"Not at all, dearest, loveliest Elizabeth," said Darcy, drawing her close again. "In my eyes, there is no other woman more worthy of being Mrs Darcy."

THE END

Sign up to the mailing list to be notified of new releases and other book news!
www.penelopeswan.com/newsletter

OTHER BOOKS BY THIS AUTHOR:

Have you read the **Dark Darcy series** ?

When Elizabeth Bennet is thrust into the path of scandal and danger, she finds unexpected assistance from the handsome but arrogant Mr Darcy. But though he may be a master at solving mysteries, what are his intentions towards her heart?

A Pride and Prejudice variation combining mystery, suspense and romance!

The Netherfield Affair (Book 1)
Intrigue at the Ball (Book 2)
The Poisoned Proposal (Book 3)
Secrets at Pemberley (Book 4)

Read an excerpt from
The Netherfield Affair:

Elizabeth awoke to the muted sounds of wind and rain. It seemed that the storm had abated—at least temporarily. Pulling her shawl around her, she hurried to the window again to look out. Now that she had the benefit of daylight, she could see that it was just as her father had described: one of the tall beech trees on the front lawn had been wrenched from its position and was now lying prone across the drive, barring the way for anyone attempting to bring a carriage or even ride a horse up to the front entrance of Longbourn.

When she went down to breakfast, however, Elizabeth learned that she had been mistaken in her supposition that a horse rider could not cross the barrier, for a message had just arrived from Netherfield Park—a letter from Jane, addressed to her.

"Well, open it, Lizzy—make haste!" said Mrs Bennet, looking up eagerly from her plate of kippers. "Perhaps it is Jane writing that Mr Bingley has proposed already!"

This elicited giggles from the younger girls and a moue of disapproval from Mary. The latter pushed her spectacles up her nose as she clasped her hands primly on the table in front of her and said:

"It behooves us to remember what is said in the Book of Proverbs 20:25: 'Marriage is based on sacred vows. Entering those vows rashly and hastily generally leads to a snare. But after you are married, it is too late to reconsider your vows'. Thus we are told that if we marry in haste, we shall repent at leisure."

"Oh Mary!" said Lydia, rolling her eyes.

Elizabeth ignored all this as she concentrated on the letter before her. It was certainly from Jane although the hand was shakier than her sister's usually beautiful penmanship. As she read the contents, Elizabeth soon understood the reason for such frail script. It appeared that Jane had taken ill and was even now awaiting a visit from Mr Jones, the apothecary, at Netherfield Park. Although Jane wrote of a simple cold, Elizabeth suspected that her gentle sister—forever concerned about giving pain to others—had made light of her illness so as not to worry her family.

"We must go and see her," declared Elizabeth with some unease.

"I would be more than happy to visit Jane, but will the carriage be able to pass the fallen tree?" asked Mrs Bennet.

Mr Bennet shook his head. "I am afraid we will not know the answer to that, my dear, until I can bring men from the farm to attempt to shift it. At present, it seems unlikely that a carriage will be able to pass. You may have to delay your visit to Jane until later today."

"I feel that I must go to Jane immediately," said Elizabeth, standing up from the table. "I shall walk to Netherfield Park."

"Walk?" gasped her mother, her eyes widening in horror. "Why, in the wind and rain... you will not be fit to be seen!"

"I shall be fit to see Jane, which is all I care about," said Elizabeth. "My mind is quite made up."

"Would you like me to ask the groom to fetch one of the horses so that you may attempt the journey on horseback?" asked Mr Bennet.

"No indeed, Papa," said Elizabeth. "It is barely three miles to Netherfield and I would welcome some fresh air after being confined indoors for so long." She glanced out of the dining room windows. "I believe that the rain has ceased for the time being and the skies look like they might be clearing. I think a refreshing walk would be the very thing."

"Have care when you arrive at Netherfield, Lizzy, for we have heard that it is haunted!" said Lydia suddenly.

Elizabeth paused and looked at her younger sister quizzically. Lydia and Kitty had been huddled together whispering for the past few minutes while Elizabeth had been discussing her plans for travelling to Netherfield, but now they hastened to inform everyone at the table of their news.

Lydia leaned forwards excitedly. "They say that there is a ghost—the spirit of a poor serving girl who was deflowered by the old master of the house many years ago—"

"Lydia!" gasped Mary.

Lydia ignored the remonstration as the rest of the table looked at her agog. She was enjoying the sensation of holding everyone's attention rapt and she was determined to make the most of her temporary advantage. "Yes, and her ghost wanders the house at night—and can even be seen sometimes looking out of the windows. On dark and stormy nights, it is possible to hear her wailing for her lost virtue and if you do not take care, she may claim your soul to keep hers company!"

"From where did you hear such an extraordinary tale?" asked Mr Bennet.

"Sarah told me," said Lydia. "And she had it directly from the Netherfield parlourmaid, who heard it from the kitchenmaid who—"

"You should know better than to listen to servants' gossip," said Elizabeth severely. "And it is well known that ghost stories are merely created to titillate and entertain. I certainly have no fear of ghoulish spirits for I do not believe that they exist."

"Aye, Lizzy," said her father with a smile. "That is a good attitude to have."

"It is not mere titillation!" insisted Lydia as Kitty nodded vehemently next to her. "Sarah told me that the servants at Netherfield have themselves observed such occurrences as to make the blood run cold—strange noises in the night, mysterious disappearances of household items, and once even a dark figure creeping up the stairs—"

"Oh! Do not talk of such things!" cried Mrs Bennet, fanning herself with her lace handkerchief. "To think of my dear Jane in such a household!"

"Perhaps now you may feel that the pursuit of Mr Bingley is not worth such gruesome risks?" enquired Mr Bennet of his wife with a teasing smile.

Mrs Bennet sniffed and looked away.

"Well, I believe that any threats that Jane may be exposed to are of an infectious rather than a supernatural variety," said Elizabeth firmly. "I thank you for the warning, Lydia, but I believe I may be safe from any ghostly attack during my visit at Netherfield."

Catching her father's twinkling eye, Elizabeth smiled, turned, and quitted the room.

Ten minutes later, Elizabeth set off on foot for Netherfield Park. She had been right in her estimation of a break in the rain, but her appraisal of the sky had been too optimistic. It did not look like it was brightening—in fact, the edges of the horizon were lined with an ominous black, which spread across the sky like an inky stain. Thick clouds loomed above, heavy with the promise of more rain, and Elizabeth hastened her steps as she cast a worried look at the heavens. It would not do to be caught in another downpour and become ill like Jane!

Elizabeth was well used to walking in the country—indeed, she enjoyed the activity immensely and indulged in it often—but today, the going was decidedly difficult. Heavy rain had turned most of the roads into a veritable quagmire and she sank up to her ankles in mud as she negotiated the stiles between the fields and attempted to avoid the puddles. She was delighted when the house at Netherfield Park finally came into view, and hastened her steps even more.

As she approached the house, Elizabeth raised her eyes to trace the outline of its elegant architecture. She had seen it several times in her rambles about the countryside and had always admired the beauty of this country manor. Today, however, it looked very different. Outlined as it was by a nimbus of black cloud in the sky behind it, the house had an almost menacing air as it sat brooding in the middle of its rain-sodden grounds.

Elizabeth laughed and chided herself for her fanciful imaginings. She was letting Lydia's wild tales and the mood of the inclement weather prevail upon her good senses, and incline her towards melodrama!

She bent her head to negotiate the last section of muddy field, then jumped as an eerie scream filled the air. Elizabeth gasped and looked around, searching for the source of the sound. Then her steps faltered as she raised her gaze once more and her eyes caught sight of something at the top of the house.

Elizabeth blinked and looked again, but she was not mistaken. There, in a small attic window, showed a ghostly white face, with black eyes that bored into her very soul.

For more information on the Dark Darcy series, go to: **www.penelopeswan.com**

(writing as **H.Y. Hanna**)

CLASSIC ROMANTIC SUSPENSE

The TENDER series

He was her first love.
Now he could be the man who wants her dead...

SWEET CONTEMPORARY ROMANCE:

Summer Beach Vets & Summer Beach Bride

Feel-good, small town beach romance
set Down Under!

For more information, go to:
www.hyhanna.com

ABOUT THE AUTHOR

Penelope Swan is the pen name of author, H.Y. Hanna, who also writes best-selling romantic suspense, mysteries and sweet romances under her other name, as well as children's fiction. She has been an avid Jane Austen fan since her teens and is delighted that she can now live out her Regency fantasies through her books. You can find out more about her and get in touch at:

www.penelopeswan.com

ACKNOWLEDGEMENTS

A huge thank you to my lovely friend, Basma, for her wonderful enthusiasm, support and feedback which has improved the story enormously. As always, I am indebted to Charles Winthrop for his loving support and encouragement for all my writing endeavours. And last but not least, to Jane Austen herself for her wonderful characters and inspiration.

Printed in Great Britain
by Amazon